IN SHADOWS WAITING

STEWART BINT

booktrope

Booktrope Editions
Seattle, WA 2015

Cover Design by Troy Johnson
Edited by Carla Barger

This is a work of fiction. Names, characters, places, brands, media, and incidents are either the product of the author's imagination or are used fictitiously. Any resemblance to similarly named places or to persons living or deceased is unintentional.

PRINT ISBN 978-1-62015-834-0
EPUB ISBN 978-1-62015-855-5
Library of Congress Control Number: 2015910161

ACKNOWLEDGMENTS

Many thanks to my Booktrope team for their hard work and dedication:

Book Manager and Marketing Manager: Majanka Verstraete

Editor: Carla Barger at BookIvy Word Studio

Cover Designer: Troy Johnson

Proofreader: Sophie Thomas

And thanks to my good friend, fellow novelist DM Cain, for her unstinting enthusiasm and encouragement.

TABLE OF CONTENTS

For my wife Sue,
and children Chris and Charlotte

CHAPTER 1: MEMORIES

Today's memories, 2014

THE CREATURE'S TRIUMPHANT LAUGH was something that would be with me until my dying day. And something I never wanted to hear again.

It was the strongest memory to stir as I looked at the photo whose colours had dimmed with age. Thirty-two years ago it was vibrant and full of life. Just like the faces staring back at me from the time before shadows. From the time before torment. From the time when we were happy.

It all reminded me of when the world was young and innocent— hell, when *I* was young and innocent. My two daughters both started sleeping with their boyfriends as soon as they turned sixteen, probably before then if the truth were told. If they had, it was something both they and my wife kept from me. But it was a different era when my sisters were that age. Helen and her Mark. Sarah and the succession of boyfriends she brought to our home, White Pastures.

I rarely smile now. Even after thirty-two years, the memories are painful. Fifty now. A half century. I was eighteen then. Yet in some ways it still seems like only yesterday.

Time plays tricks.

A tear rolls down my cheek.

* * *

Earlier memories, 1983

AS SARAH WHIRLED to face me, I caught sight of the sheepish grin that always crept over her full ruby lips whenever she felt guilty.

"Simon!" she laughed, hesitantly. "I. . .I was just. . ." She faltered as she followed my gaze to the photograph gripped in her left hand. In the split second before she turned back to the window I glimpsed tears in her deep blue eyes, and put my arm comfortingly around her shoulders.

Gently, I eased the picture from her grasp and looked at the two faces framed there, captured twelve months earlier by the portrait lens of Dad's Pentax. One could have been Sarah five years into the future—the same silky blonde hair tumbled past the shoulders, the same impish eyes and smiling mouth. The only difference was that the cheeks in the photo showed a trace of blusher and the eyelids a hint of misty blue. There was no mistaking the girl in the picture for anyone other than Sarah's older sister.

The second face, pressed tightly against the girl's, featured sad brown eyes, a long tapering black nose, and a body entirely covered with rusty hair. Our poor red setter, Titus, had always posed beautifully when he saw a camera.

I glanced up through the window to the young cherry tree flourishing at the side of the lawn, hinting its intention to tower strong and firm in years to come. It marked Titus's grave. We had buried him in the part of the garden where he loved to play and planted the tree in his memory.

This was not the first time I had found Sarah standing at her bedroom window, photograph in hand, looking out at the tree, and I could guess what was going through her mind. Not only did it remind us of happier times, it also served to recall the full horror our family had recently come through.

The horror that began on the day of my final A level examination.

CHAPTER 2: FIRST COMING

I BURST THROUGH the lounge door and flopped into my favourite chair, flinging my jacket across the settee.

"Hi, Sarah," I called above the noise of the television. My sister lay on her stomach on the floor, her bare legs waving in the air as one of *The Tomorrow People* got himself out of another tricky situation.

"Hi, Simon. How'd it go today?"

"Okay. I think I did well enough. That last-minute revision on the 1974 coal strike paid off. It actually came up."

Sarah pulled a face. "Spare me the details, please. And remind me not to take modern history. By the way, what time are you going out tonight?"

"I don't think I am. I reckon I've earned a rest. Goodbye A levels. Hello relaxation."

"You're not going to be cluttering up the house, are you? With Mum and Dad out tonight, I was hoping Steve could come round."

"Steve?"

"I met him at the disco last weekend. I did tell you about him."

The protective instinct in me took over. "Well, I'm definitely not going out now. I'm not leaving you alone in the house with any Steve."

Sarah shot me her well-rehearsed look of exasperation. "Simon, I *am* fourteen. And anyway, we won't be alone. Helen'll be in."

"Sorry, but I'm staying in front of the telly. I want to catch up on a few videos I haven't had time to watch."

"I thought you said you'd be going out to celebrate once your A levels were over?"

"And so I am, just not tonight, clever clogs." I hurled a cushion at her that she warded off expertly.

"Well shut up then and let me watch this," she said. *The Tomorrow People* had always been one of her favourites.

Lying back in the chair, I felt as if all the cares of the world had suddenly been lifted from my shoulders, and I remembered how excited my older sister, Helen, had been when she got home after her last A level a couple of years ago.

Freedom at last!

I can't recall the exact time it started, but dusk was just beginning to make its presence felt, and we were thinking of drawing the curtains. Helen and I had followed Sarah and Steve into the lounge straight after dinner. Then Sarah had taken Steve upstairs about a quarter of an hour earlier to practice a new dance routine, meaning that my schlock horror video was competing with the dull thudding of "Take That" booming from her bedroom stereo.

It might have been the flicker of a cloud scurrying in front of the sun's dying embers that sent the sudden dark shadow past the window. I blinked and sat bolt upright. Helen turned towards me with a quizzical look. Her corn-blond hair fell loosely about her shoulders.

"Did you see that?" she asked.

I nodded slowly. "I thought I saw someone go by the window."

She swallowed nervously. No doubt she was remembering the spate of burglaries in the village during the last couple of months.

The movement had almost convinced me that someone was in the garden. Trying to appear nonchalant, I got up and peered out into the fading light. There was no sign of anyone, and an intruder would have had to scale an eight-foot wall or break down the door between the garage and house.

But I didn't want to take any chances. As I made my way into the dining room, Helen moved across to the lounge window. I pulled open the patio doors and stepped outside, suddenly feeling queasy and wishing I'd brought Titus. He was in the kitchen, though, and if I went back for him an intruder would have plenty of time to get away.

Everywhere I looked half-shadows and shafts of almost ethereal light filtered through the trees and bushes.

"Who's there?" I called, not really expecting an answer—and definitely not hoping for one. When none came, I knew I had been misled by the strange half-light of the dusk. I shivered for no apparent reason, other than someone possibly walking over my grave, and thought it was getting rather chilly for what had been an overpoweringly hot day.

I stepped back inside, drew the doors shut and turned the key, double-checking that they were locked.

"No one there," I said jauntily, as I walked back to the lounge and settled down again in front of the television.

The video was full of typical schlock horror garbage of machete-wielding maniacs chasing innocent girls through the woods. I wondered why the girls were always barefoot with their hands tied behind their backs. Still, the storyline was better than most and the excitement continued to mount.

In fact, it was so exciting that Helen dozed off. Thank goodness she did, or she would probably have seen the face at the window before it vanished as quickly as it had come.

I leaped up, stifling a yell, but the face had already melted away into the thickening gloom.

Had I really seen it? It had been too indistinct for me to make out any features. It was more a shape than anything, but it was the shape of a figure nevertheless.

Without waking Helen, I went out through the dining room patio doors again, but, just as before, I could see no one. This time I painstakingly searched the far reaches of the garden for more than five minutes, every nook and cranny, behind every tree and bush. By the time I was satisfied that I was definitely alone, the half-light had turned into early night, but the rising moon kept full darkness at bay.

On the way back inside, I paused at the door—just a step away from the threshold of safety—to take a last lingering look around. Nothing. But I had seen something out there, hadn't I? What about Helen? She'd seen something, too, hadn't she?

* * *

The next day Dad looked puzzled when I told him what had happened.

"That's odd," he said. "I thought I saw something a couple of times last week when you were upstairs revising. But each time I went out to have a look there was nothing there. What was it you saw, exactly?"

"Not really sure how to describe it. Just a sort of fleeting movement that I only glimpsed out of the corner of my eye."

"Yeah, that's it, that's all I saw. Just a flicker, and then it was gone. Perhaps it's just that time of year, something to do with the sun setting behind the trees."

He'd been talking about getting tighter security for the last few weeks, especially after our neighbours were burgled, and I tried to look beyond his smiling eyes to see if he was merely trying to reassure me. But there was no hint that he did not firmly believe what he was saying.

That evening I set out for my schoolfriend's house. I'd arranged to meet him at seven o'clock, and we were going on to meet more friends at a club in town. It was a fabulous night, though a little hazy when it came to remembering exactly what we'd got up to.

After the club we went back to my friend's house for a few final beers. It was four in the morning when I found myself slipping my key in the lock at home. I crept in and turned to face the door as I gently pushed it shut.

At that moment, something brushed my shoulder. Had my throat not instantly locked with fear, the yell of fright that wanted to explode from my body would have awoken the entire house. As it was, the only sound was my heart pounding, pumping vast quantities of adrenalin through my bloodstream. Summoning all the courage I could, I slowly turned.

"Helen! What did you want to scare me like that for?"

"Sorry," she hissed urgently, "but I had to see you before you went to bed."

The distraught look on her face told me something was wrong. Very wrong. Her independent nature usually overrode what she normally thought of as irrational fears.

"What is it? Do Mum and Dad know you're still up?"

"No. I went upstairs early and lay awake listening for them to go to bed. I hoped they'd be asleep before you came in."

Suddenly it all came gushing out. "Simon. It came again tonight. It wasn't the sun, I know it wasn't. The whole window darkened for a split second, but when I turned to look there was no one there."

"Did Mum and Dad see it?"

Slowly Helen nodded. "Dad did. He had a good look all around the garden but there was no sign of anyone."

I feared that nothing I could do or say would ease the torment she was clearly going through. "Just like the other time. I wonder if we're not imagining it." I was aware that the vodka and beer (more than I cared to even try to remember) were slurring my voice and blunting my thought process. "After all, we haven't actually—"

"I know what I saw"—her interruption was sharp and scathing—"and I thought you did, as well."

"I saw a movement outside the window, that's all. It could have been anything."

Her eyes were daggers, and a voice inside me was a nagging reminder that I was as worried as she was. *What about that face at the window?* it said. *That was more than a fleeting movement.*

"No burglar in his right mind is going to break in while everyone's in the house," I said, trying hard to shut out the fear. "It's very common to see flickers of light or shadow as the sun's going down."

The inner voice persisted. *But the face. There was a face at the window. You know there was. You saw it.*

Okay, so I know it was a face, but talking about it wouldn't make Helen feel any better. In fact, it would only make things worse.

The liquid contents of my stomach felt as if they were on the verge of making a desperate bid for freedom.

"I suppose you're right," said Helen, pulling herself up, as if a ramrod-straight back would ward off any intruder. "But at the time it was so real, and I felt so peculiar, so horribly alone."

Her words cut no ice with me. I knew that deep down she didn't believe what she was saying. Just as if she were trying to reassure me with the same lie that I was using to convince her. And the strange thing was that "horribly alone" was exactly how I had felt, too. It was the first time my feelings had been put into words; her description defined it perfectly. Horribly alone. Yes, that was it to a T, even though Helen had been with me at the time.

"Do you want me to take a look around?" I asked, attempting to make the situation seem as normal as possible even though all I wanted to do was get my head inside the toilet bowl.

"It was hours ago," she replied, her face pleading with me to go, no matter what she said. "Whoever it was will be long gone."

"If it'll make you feel better. . ."

She bit her bottom lip. "I suppose you might see some sign of where he got over the wall. But do be careful."

I nodded. I wanted to take Titus but he was asleep.

I walked into the dining room and picked up the decorative poker that lay in the fireplace. Gently pulling back the curtain, I drew the patio door open.

As I listened intently, the warm night air seemed almost alive somehow, yet nothing stirred. Peering into the darkness, my vision was aided by the stars, which helped penetrate to the far reaches of the garden.

All was quiet. All was still. The leaves hung silent in the trees. It was a cloying, claustrophobic night, no breath of air or wind anywhere. The warmth snuggled up to me, yet still I shivered. *Nerves*, I told myself angrily. *Just nerves. There's no one out here. Except me.*

I took three steps beyond the door, then four, five, six. I turned and looked back at Helen silhouetted in the brilliant light flooding through the open doorway. It seemed more than ordinary light surrounded her. Her outline appeared to have a bluish tint, and it radiated fiercely into the darkness.

A bush alongside me rustled and moved. Suppressing my natural instinct to scream—screams seemed to be building inside me that night with nowhere to go—I whirled round just in time to see a black shape dart out from under the bush, streak across the grass, and disappear into the undergrowth.

"Bloody cats," I hissed, but I had to smile. When I turned and looked at Helen a couple of seconds later, the blue aura had gone, leaving her framed in a more ordinary light. This was just before my stomach growled, erupting a volcano of beer, vodka, and curry into the bush.

By the time the lava well ran dry and there was nothing left for the painful retching to expel, Helen had gone inside.

CHAPTER 3: THE GROWING THING

SEEING SARAH AND HELEN wander downstairs and out into the garden in their bikinis reminded me that I ought to start getting used to the sun before going on holiday.

I spent the afternoon lying on the lawn with the girls reading a book. Or trying to. My thoughts refused to stay with the printed word, turning instead to the events of the last couple of nights. My mind's eye tried to picture the exact shape or movement of the thing I had seen, but it proved an impossible task because there hadn't really been anything tangible to it. I stared at the spot where I thought I'd seen it, and felt angry with myself for doing so.

I told myself that it was just the spate of burglaries getting under my skin, making me jumpy and causing me to read something into the situation that wasn't really there. Mum hadn't seen anything, neither had Sarah. In that bright June sunshine, it all seemed so far away and impossible, so why did I get the feeling that once the sun went down it would be back? Both times all I'd seen was one single movement for a fleeting half second. So why on Earth was I getting so worked up about it? *The burglaries*, said the voice. *That's why.*

The fact that Helen had seen it too and, more importantly, perhaps, had seemed so troubled by it was one reason why I needed to take it seriously. But how could I take it seriously if I couldn't even see it?

A warm summer's breeze began to stir the leaves.

Mum and Dad went for a long walk with Titus, and that evening the three of them seemed worn out. Normally Titus wasn't allowed in the lounge, but somehow he crept in while we were having dinner. After dinner we found him in the lounge, curled up in front of the hearth fast asleep. No one had the heart to wake him. Mum and Dad were tired. Even Sarah was drowsy. But I caught a glance from Helen and knew I wouldn't be dropping asleep in the lounge. I doubted she would, either.

It's all so unreasonable, I thought. *It's only a shadow. Why do I feel so uncomfortable about it?*

I tried to concentrate on the film, but all the time my eyes were drawn—as if by some unseen magnet—to the window. I dragged them away, glancing at the television before looking across the room at Helen. Her eyes, too, seemed directed to the window.

Even before it became dark, I'd had enough. I was starting to imagine all sorts of things. As soon as the sun began to lose its power and kiss the treetops, I leaped up and hurried over to the window.

Helen fixed me with a wide-eyed stare as I swiftly drew the curtains. Rubbing my hands together, I strolled back to the chair.

"Cosier this way," I explained as I settled down to the film again.

Titus often wagged his tail in his sleep (perhaps dreaming of chasing cats or rabbits) but this time it was accompanied by a low growl. Suddenly he was wide awake; he jerked his head off the rug and glanced at us one by one as if to make sure we were all still there. He stood up stiffly, his tail firmly between his legs.

"What's up, old boy?" I held my hand out to him. "Did you have a bad dream? Get beaten up by a cat?"

Without moving, he stared intently at the window. Immediately I felt my hackles rise and a shiver ran along my spine.

"Oh God," muttered Helen under her breath.

In one bound Titus was at the window, barking loud enough to wake the dead and pawing crazily at the curtains. I flung myself across the room and pulled them back. For a split second I saw a dark movement outside. Titus turned and ran to the door. He flopped down heavily, alternating between panting and whining in a high-pitched tone.

The shape, whatever it was, was gone. All was now still. Had I seen it or not? I looked at Titus. He stared at me as I stood by the window. But was it me he was looking at? It struck me that perhaps his gaze went beyond me and out to the garden. To something wandering amongst the trees.

My dash to the window had yanked everyone out of their own private reverie, so when I swept the curtain aside they all saw what I saw.

Throughout it all, Helen had sat completely still. But now the spell was broken; tears rolled uncontrollably down her cheeks, and she was shaking violently.

"It was there again. I saw it," she sobbed. "Just for a split second, but I did see it." Mum ran over to her in a flash and comforted her. Sarah just lay on the floor not saying a word. She didn't need to. The look in her eyes told me that she had seen it too.

Mum turned from Helen's chair and looked at Dad. "There was someone out there, Bob," she said firmly. "I saw him."

Dad was pale, definitely not like him. Nodding thoughtfully, he said, "Yes, I saw something out there, as well."

In some ways it was a relief to know I wasn't going crazy, but this incident made it real and therefore deadly serious. Someone was outside and had been before. A strained silence rang throughout the room until Titus ran to the window, barking furiously.

"Come on, boy," I cried instinctively, heading for the dining room. I opened the patio doors and out we went, Titus flying like the wind across the lawn with me in as close pursuit as my two human legs would allow. The gods lent speed to my heels, and I quickly arrived at his side as he stood clawing angrily at the foot of the wall.

Then suddenly, footsteps behind me. I whirled around. Dad stood behind me with a torch, which he aimed at the soil at the base of the wall.

"No one here," I said.

"And no footprints either. Surely there'd be something here if anyone had climbed over the wall." Dad shone the light all about us, peering closely at the trees and bushes. Nothing appeared to have been disturbed.

"I'm going to ring the police," he said. "It's time they knew about this."

Slowly we walked towards the welcoming glow just inside the patio doors, but Titus was reluctant to come, and instead ran furiously around the lawn barking.

"Come on, Titus," I called from the door. "No one is there now." He inched his way towards the house, tail still between his legs. Then he stopped a couple of yards away. A dangerous growl seeped through his bared teeth.

"Titus, what is it?"

His eyes fixed on the door and he crouched as if ready to pounce. I took a couple of steps towards him, but the increased growling warned me it would be better to stay away. He seemed to be staring past me into the dining room.

*   *   *

"I've been over every inch of your garden, Mr. Reynolds," the police officer said, switching off his torch as he stood framed in the open doorway. "There's no sign of an intruder and no indication that anyone's been over the wall. I think you're all clear."

Dad looked embarrassed. "I'm sorry to have bothered you. But with all these burglaries in the village. . ."

"No trouble at all, sir. Better to be safe than sorry. And if you see anyone else please let us know straight away. We're anxious to follow every lead we can get at the moment."

"Thank you very much, Constable. We're grateful you came, anyway."

"Pleasure, sir. And if it'll put your mind at rest we'll keep an eye on the house for the next couple of days. You never know. We might just spot something."

*   *   *

The next day I was alone in the house. Dad at work, Sarah at school, Mum visiting friends, and Helen at her office where she was training to be an estate agent. I spent the morning lazing about my room listening to CDs, and in the afternoon I wrote a few sheets to a girlfriend who lived up North.

Sarah was at the age when she would fall madly in love with every good-looking boy she came across, and a constant stream of callers came for her. Neither Dad nor I could keep track of her boyfriends; no sooner had we got used to one and were able to remember his name than he was out on his ear and there was another smiling face at the door. And the funny thing was, Mum and Helen never seemed to notice the difference. All Mum would say when she went to the door was, "Come in, dear. She won't be a minute." And Helen had her nose too far into her own love life to be worried about little sister.

The police kept watch over the house all day. I noticed the blue Escort parked across the road when I nipped to the chippy for lunch. Two men were sitting in it, one reading a paper, the other doing a crossword. And for a moment I felt a little guilty that we may have been wasting police time.

We'd discussed that very point after the constable left the previous night. The feeling that someone was prowling about the garden had left almost as quickly as it had come. The thoughts and doubts lingered, certainly, but the actual prickly feeling that an intruder was present had simply disappeared.

Sarah went out that evening with Steve while Mum and Dad went to an environmental health officers' summer dinner dance, leaving Helen and me in the house alone.

I was determined that if the prowler came again I would see him properly this time. Television was its usual boring summer self so it was no real hardship to sit staring at the window. But as darkness pulled its cloak slowly over the light and warmth of the day, I began to imagine all sorts of movements in the trees.

The television droned on in the background and my eyelids started to droop. As I shook my head to clear the cobwebs that were beginning to envelop my mind, I continued my vigil, not daring to look away from that one spot in the window in case the thing returned. I didn't want to miss the second or two I would need to prove that someone was out there.

Darkness descended swiftly once dusk took a foothold. The night shrouded the house like a veil, seemingly deeper and closer than usual. I knew in my soul that whoever was watching us was simply biding his time. I risked a quick sideways look towards Helen and saw that she too had fixed her stare on the window. She seemed to have sensed my glance because she cast a reassuring smile in my direction. Suddenly a single bark rang out from the kitchen where Titus had been stretched out on the floor. Helen jerked her head towards the window, and I involuntarily looked across at her. It was at that precise moment that she screamed.

Instead of looking back at the window as I should have done, my gaze remained locked on Helen. Her hands flew to her face, covering her mouth, gripping both sides of her nose; her eyes were wide with a look of pure terror, as if she were witnessing the ultimate horror.

It's strange the things that pass through your mind during a time of crisis. I remember that time seemed to stand still while obscenities circled my vocal chords waiting for me to give them life. I'd done what it —whatever IT was—wanted. Somehow, it had caused me to look away and then appeared as soon as I was distracted.

I knew it was too late, but I turned to the window nevertheless, a shiver still tingling my spine. Again, just a hint of a dark shadow seemed to kill the moonlight, but I was aware of something—just for a split second—looking in, waiting to devour us with its evil.

At least, that's how I felt. It was the feeling of intense horror— deep, penetrating, and powerful—that engulfed me so suddenly, rather than the sight of the thing that was so terrifying and loathsome. It seemed an eternity before I could shake it off sufficiently to regain control of my senses. Titus barked furiously. We could hear him scratching frantically at the door.

The darkness at the window had disappeared as swiftly as it had come and the next second I was heading for the door. I ran through the dining room towards the kitchen where Titus was still in a frenzy. For an instant the door refused to yield to my pushing, conjuring up all sorts of visions—it was in the kitchen, waiting. It had come inside to get us.

I was now more determined than ever to see this thing, whatever it was—burglar, shadow, menace—and I battered the door with all my strength. A squeal of pain and muffled thumping gave me a quick sense of satisfaction as the door met with resistance, connecting with whoever was in there.

As I burst inside my hand snaked up the wall toward the light switch giving life to the overhead fluorescent strip. Realisation dawned on me immediately, partly because of the silence and partly because of the sight: I had slammed the door into poor Titus who had been leaping up on it. Sad brown eyes looked out from the tangled mass of head, legs and hair as he rolled over and scrambled to his feet.

"Oh, sorry, Titus. Sorry, old boy." He whined and licked my outstretched hand. Then, suddenly, he snatched his head away and turned to face the door that led out into the garden. A wave shuddered along the hair on his back and a low growl was born in the pit of his stomach.

"What is it?" I asked myself as much as the dog. His answer was to shoot away from me, skidding to a halt at the garden door. As he stared up at it, his growling became more urgent and insistent. As soon as he saw me reach for the handle he started pawing at the door. It was hardly open more than a crack when his nose poked through, and with a deft twist of his head he sent the door flying from my grasp.

As I followed him out into the moonlight, I caught sight of him as he disappeared round the side of the house towards the back garden, barking more frantically all the time. An eerie light washed over the stretch of lawn giving rise to the illusion of a rippling lake, a lake of grass flanked by elms and sycamores with a copse at the end.

On rounding the corner of the house, I finally saw it. Titus was chasing a running figure that was partly blending in with the moonlit shadows of the trees.

Although it seemed to be running, I couldn't actually see its legs moving. Its speed, though, told me it must be sprinting. As my eyes grew more accustomed to the darkness, I saw the figure stop and turn to face Titus, who by then was only a couple of metres behind it. All I could make out was a black shape advancing slowly, threateningly, menacingly, towards my dog. Titus drew himself up as if he had hit an invisible wall and a howl of horror wrenched from his body. Turning tail, he hurtled back towards me across the lawn. His pursuer came rapidly out of the shadows but was too far away for me to discern any of its features. I could still only make out a vague black shape.

Almost at once I sensed that it saw me because it glided to a halt. There we stood, forty metres of lawn between us like two duelling cowboys at high noon. A faint moaning came from its direction, then without warning, it rose about ten feet up into the air and began to grow, both in height and in width. It moved slowly through the darkness, expanding constantly like some huge, obscene balloon until I felt sure it meant to engulf me. I stood frozen to the spot, as if my feet had taken root, my eyes locked on the shadow.

I'm not seeing this, I told myself. *I can't be seeing this. It isn't happening.*

The spell holding me paralysed was broken by a piercing scream from the house. I spun to face the lounge window and saw Helen's terror-stricken face framed in the glass staring out into the night. A faint rustling came from above me and when I turned back to where the shadow had been hovering there was no sign of it.

Sweat poured down my forehead as I ran back to the house and slammed the door behind me. Titus was under the table whining. Not far away from him was a wet pool where he had been sick on the floor. Helen rushed into the kitchen and fell into my arms sobbing. "What was it?" she cried.

I clasped her to me as tightly as I could. "It was nothing," I lied. "Only a shadow. That's all."

She pushed me away angrily. "That was no shadow. You know it wasn't. You saw it. It was a. . . a. . . a. . ." Her words refused to come. Like me, she could find no reasonable explanation for what we had just seen. The expression she had used previously—*horribly alone*—sprang to mind again. My senses as well as my eyes told me this thing was not of this world. No mortal could have instilled the sense of horror that the faceless dark shadow, that growing thing, had. The only evidence we had was that of our own eyes and our own feelings. I began to wonder whether we would have to rely on feelings and intuition alone in our future dealings with this unwelcome visitor. Whatever it was.

CHAPTER 4: MARK

GROANING, I TURNED AWAY from the luminous readout on my clock radio. Normally I slept until the alarm sounded but I woke in the middle of the night and lay there for hours. I had a lot on my mind. I'd almost convinced myself that our mysterious visitor was supernatural. Had someone told me a few days ago that I'd be rationally making out that we had a ghost at home I'd have laughed in their faces, but now it didn't seem too outrageous. Actually, it seemed to be the only explanation to fit the facts. That shadow was real. The way it had grown was a fact. The way Titus reacted to it was a fact. The way it terrified the living daylights out of Helen and me was very much a fact.

But why should we be so frightened? (*Horribly alone*, said the inner voice. *Horribly alone*.) It had certainly left a most peculiar feeling when it appeared at the window, but it hadn't hurt me in the garden, had it? (That nagging inner voice again: *waiting to devour us with its evil*.) *People talk a lot of nonsense about ghosts and spirits*, I said to myself as I turned over. *Surely something that's not of this world can't harm us. Now, had it been a burglar there would be real cause to be frightened. Burglars can shoot us, stab us, hit us over the head with a vase. But what could an ethereal ghost do, especially from outside the house?*

The thought that the ghost was outside the house must have been in my mind when I finally fell asleep because in my nightmare the ghost got inside. I was in the kitchen with Helen when the carving knife suddenly flew through the air and plunged deep into Helen's heart. She fell silently to the floor.

I woke in a cold sweat and sat bolt upright. It took a few seconds to remember where I was and to realise that it was just a nightmare. I glanced at the clock. Quarter past four.

I flopped down again and made up my mind that the thing wasn't going to intimidate me. As long as it was outside the house, just passing by the window, it was harmless. And if it did put in a longer appearance, who knew, I might even be able to talk to it, find out what it wanted, perhaps find out more about life on the other side of the mystical veil of death. I almost shook with excitement. A ghost could be quite fun, couldn't it, just as long as I didn't let the creepy side of the situation get to me?

I don't know what made me get out of bed and wander to the window other than an eerie compulsion. Poking my head between the curtains, I peered into the moonlight and saw the garden stretching away into a mass of trees and bushes. At first all was quiet and still. Not a sound anywhere. Then I saw a patch of darkness appear. With the moon overhead, the night was quite bright. My eyes focused on the bottom of the garden, the place where traditionally fairies have always played. There were no fairies now. Instead, a dreadful feeling of unease washed over me, ignoring all my attempts to dispel it.

Something stirred in the bushes. Only faintly, but there was a definite movement. It was then, when my eyes were trained like those of a hawk into the very heart of the bushes, that I saw a dark shape flit through the moonlight. For just one agonisingly fleeting second, I glimpsed the shape of a man running, then it was gone without a trace even though there was nowhere for it to go except into thin air. In that same second the eerie feeling also disappeared, just as if it had been his all-embracing cloak and he had taken it with him to keep him warm in his abominable lair.

*   *   *

Over the next few days I came to accept—and indeed expect—our visitor. He put in an appearance each evening just as the sun began to go watery and sink behind the treetops. I suppose I was a trifle blasé about it but it no longer frightened me. It hadn't hurt us and seemed content to flit harmlessly past the window and roam amongst the shrubs and trees.

I awoke late on Saturday feeling somewhat cheated. There I was, a gentleman of leisure idling away my days in the sun, taking things easy, and now it was Saturday when everyone else could laze about too. Looking through the bedroom window, I saw Helen and Sarah already stretched out in their bikinis.

A mischievous grin creased my face as I strolled into the garden wearing my pale blue trunks with the vivid red flash across the front. The time had come to tease poor Helen mercilessly. Such is brotherly love.

"Today's the day," I chanted. "Today's the day."

Helen looked up warily as I laid my towel down beside her. "If you're going to behave like a child go and sunbathe somewhere else," she said. "Anyway, Sarah's already beaten you to it."

Sarah lifted her head and gave me a slight wink; we'd rehearsed the next bit. "Who's got stars in her eyes," we chorused together. "Today's the day, today's the day."

Helen smiled and sunk back down, refusing to take our bait. Her boyfriend, Mark Brody, was coming to stay for a fortnight and I knew she could hardly wait.

She seemed a different girl today. Despite my reassurances about our mysterious visitor, she had been taking it hard and her cheeks had grown pale, contrasting with the dark bags that had appeared under her eyes. I suspected she wasn't sleeping, for days she was nervous and on edge. But now everything had changed. She was starting a couple of weeks' holiday, was bubbly and vibrant, and had carelessly tossed our teasing aside. What an effect Mark was having on her and he hadn't even arrived yet. I hardly dared to hope that he would bring her back to normal.

Eventually the magical time arrived when she was able to set off to meet his train. The sun blazed down as I pulled myself up on one elbow and drank deeply from my bottle of lager. I lay back again and stretched luxuriously, rubbing my shoulders from side to side on the slightly rough surface of the towel while I watched Helen pull on her shorts and sandals.

"Bye. See you in a bit," she called cheerfully as she headed towards the wooden door that lead to the drive. A few moments later we heard her revving the engine of Mum's Nissan, a crackle of churned gravel, and then she was gone, out on to the quiet road down to the station.

Sarah scrambled up. "Simon, while Helen's away I want to show you something."

"What?" I was puzzled. This was unexpected.

"Her birthday present. Come and look."

"But it's ages to her birthday."

"No it's not. It's only a week away. Come and see what I've got her."

I groaned inwardly. Only a week! How could I have forgotten? I thought I had at least two weeks to get her something.

"Very nice," I said as I stood in Sarah's bedroom fingering the ruby-red velvet covering of the jewellery box that she had thrust into my hands. "But what am I supposed to get her?" I said it more to myself than to Sarah, but she giggled.

"Well, I thought you might like to get her something to go in it." She reached down into the open drawer and pulled out a sparkling gold necklace. "Something like this, for instance."

I took the plaited serpentine chain and held it up to the window where the sun glinted brightly on it.

Sarah looked at me expectantly. "If you like it, you owe me £22. If not, I'll take it back and you can get her something yourself."

She giggled again as I reached out to ruffle her hair. How well my sisters knew me.

"Of course I like it. If you think she'll like it, that is?"

"She'll love it. She was admiring it in the jeweller's last week. Dropping hints, I think."

"I owe you £22."

"I thought you might say that."

* * *

The commotion in the drive told me Helen was back with Mark. I liked Mark Brody, and as soon as I saw him appear through the door with Helen's beaming face just behind I felt sure my sister would soon settle down and we would begin to enjoy the summer.

Mark strode over to me. "Simon, how are you?" Gripping his outstretched hand, I looked into the carefree blue eyes and at the meticulously-kept blond hair that flowed over his ears. The last time

I had seen him was a couple of months earlier at his twenty-first birthday party.

"I'm fine, thanks, Mark." I glanced heavenward. "Let's hope this wonderful weather stays while you're here."

He hoisted aloft a small brown leather bag. "I sure hope it does," he said, grinning. "I'm travelling light. Trunks and more trunks, to say nothing of a couple of pairs of shorts."

During dinner that night he was his usual chatty self, talking virtually nonstop. Helen's rapturous gaze hardly left his face. Suddenly, as the meal was ending, I saw Mark's head jerk slightly. A slight frown creased his high forehead as his eyes turned momentarily towards the dining room window. At that particular moment Dad was almost at the punchline of one of his jokes and all eyes apart from mine were on him. I had been splitting my attention between Dad and the window, waiting for the shadow to come again. We started dinner rather late, and I knew it would return before we finished. Again, it seemed that the thing had drawn my eyes back into the room before making its usual dash past the window. I was looking across the table at Mark, praying he would be my sister's salvation, when he shot a puzzled glance past her into the twilight.

Breathing a silent curse, I jerked my head around and pushed back in my chair.

I sighed as I peered out into the gloom. I was so frustrated. Something had definitely gone past the window, but as before, I had only caught a glimpse of it. Mark quickly recovered his composure and laughed perfectly in time with the end of Dad's joke. I knew he had seen something, yet there was nothing on his smiling face to indicate that he had.

How I envied him. All through my life my face has reflected my true feelings—and landed me in hot water on more occasions than I care to remember! Narrowing my eyes, I peered hard into his face. He caught my quizzical stare and held my eyes firmly for a couple of seconds. Then he wrenched himself away and turned to smile at Helen. She was still laughing from Dad's joke and had obviously seen nothing pass the window, nor had she seen what transpired between Mark and me. It was at that moment that Titus let out a howl from the kitchen. I shot a warning glance at Mark, sensing he was about to tell what he had seen outside.

"I'll see to him," I said, pushing my chair back and getting up quickly.

"I'll come too," said Helen, a troubled look playing across her previously carefree face. Together we went into the kitchen to find our poor pet cowering in a corner.

"Titus, old feller, what's the matter?" He lethargically licked my outstretched hand as his sad and questioning eyes looked for solace in my touch. Helen shut the door behind us and crouched down alongside me. Titus turned his attention to her as she ticked behind his ears.

"Simon, was it there again?" Her voice was so tinged with terror that I didn't have the heart to do anything except nod blankly.

Before she could answer my silent gesture, a shout came from the dining room. It was Mark's voice, but his words were indistinct. The next moment it seemed that all hell in its potent fury had broken forth. A chair crashed over, Sarah screamed, and Dad uttered an uncharacteristically Anglo-Saxon phrase.

Titus leaped up and his tail lashed back and forth as he pawed at the door. Rushing forward, I pulled it open. As we tumbled through into the dining room Dad was halfway to the patio door while everyone else peered out of the window into the rapidly fading light.

Mark turned from the window and strode after Dad. "I'll come, too." He hurried out without as much as a glance at the rest of us.

"What's happened?" cried Helen.

"There's someone out there." Mum's voice quivered a little. "Mark saw a face at the window."

A shiver ran down my spine as I turned to Helen, our eyes meeting. I knew Mark had caught my warning glance earlier and I felt an irrational stab of anger over his irresponsibility at creating a fuss over a shadow flitting past the window. I rushed out into the growing gloom of the garden, catching Mark's arm. "What did you see, Mark?" I demanded of him.

"I saw whoever you saw just before Titus cried out," he said, shaking off my hand and hurrying after Dad once more.

I caught his arm again and pulled him back. "And then?"

His voice had a touch of reticence. "While you and Helen were with the dog I got a feeling we were being watched. I looked over to the window and there was a face looking in. He glared at us and his features seemed to twist with hatred. I've never seen anything like it. I shouted out and he simply disappeared. Just vanished into thin air."

It was no use trying to tell him the truth. I was sure he wouldn't believe in ghosts and things that went bump in the night. I wasn't quite so sure myself now. Was it human after all? Could it just be a prowler waiting for the chance to break in?

Something rushed past me, brushing my trousers. Startled, I looked down, then shuddered with relief as Titus tore out into the night.

"We'd better go and help Dad," I said, reluctant to think any more about it for the moment. "If there are prowlers we can't let him be out there by himself."

Following five minutes of searching that revealed nothing, I suggested to Mark that he go back to see that Helen and the others were alright. "We did leave the door open," I said. "If anyone's about they could have got in."

He hurried off across the lawn and I stood on the very spot where, just for one fleeting moment, I had seen the running figure a couple of nights ago. Dad looked at me expectantly, as if sensing I had got rid of Mark for a reason.

"A face at the window now, eh?" I said. I hadn't told Dad about my close encounter with the growing shadow the other night, thinking he'd consider me stupid or irrational or, of course, quite possibly drunk, based on the excesses of my end-of-A-level celebrations.

He looked at me curiously, perhaps catching my faraway look. "What is it?" he asked. "There's something you're not telling me."

I nodded. "It seems so silly. It wasn't silly at the time, though. It was quite frightening when it was actually happening."

Dad inclined his head, waiting silently for me to continue.

"The thing is," I said. "Helen saw it too. It was that night you went to the council dinner dance."

"The night you said Titus was sick?"

"Yes. I told you I didn't know what made him sick. That's not quite true."

Dad listened without changing his expression while I related the events of that night, leaving nothing out.

"And you say Helen saw it too?"

"Yes. I'm getting worried about her, Dad."

There was a pause of several seconds, then he fixed me with his gaze again. "And you think Mark's just seen the same thing?"

"Well, he must have. It would make sense, wouldn't it? I caught a glimpse of something—that snatch of movement we saw before."

"But the face?"

"I didn't see that."

Dad looked at me long and hard for what seemed like an eternity. "Simon," he said, averting his eyes, an unusual hint of hesitancy in his voice, "are we really crazy enough to think this is a ghost?"

I nodded. "I think I am, anyway. Don't ask me why, but I get such a peculiar feeling of uncertainty when it's about. I know it sounds stupid, but that's how it is."

"This face at the window is a bit different though," said Dad. "It could be trying something new on us."

"Unless Mark is the only one who can see its features." *Am I really having a rational conversation with my Dad in our garden about ghosts?* I wondered incredulously. "Not everyone is supposed to be able to see ghosts. Oh, I wish I knew more about them. I'll go to the library on Monday and see if I can find any books on the supernatural."

"And another thing," mused Dad, "why us? And why has it suddenly started to come now?"

They were questions to which we had no answers. Yet.

CHAPTER 5: COMMUNICATION

THE FOLLOWING EVENING we decided to let Titus be with us. If it comes again, we reasoned, Titus will feel it first and put us on our guard. During dinner he lay by the stone fireplace when he suddenly started the same low-pitched growl as the previous week when he'd sensed the thing in the garden. I turned to the window instantly. This time there was no mistake: a shadow had passed the window. At walking pace. The shadow of a man. Then it disappeared and all was calm and peaceful in my mind, as before. But I had seen it much more clearly this time.

Just as I was looking away, an insane shiver gripped my spine, refusing to let go—*Horribly alone. Waiting to devour us with its evil*—and bringing with it the same feelings I'd had when it was with us before. But it wasn't with us now, was it? It had come and gone. *You saw it properly this time, though,* the inner voice told me, *and that's why you still feel horribly alone. You know it's out there somewhere. Waiting to devour you with its evil.*

Mark's hand shot out and pointed accusingly at the window. "Look there," he cried.

But there's nothing there, I wanted to shout. *Nothing at all. You've missed it. It was there a minute ago. But now it's gone.*

As Titus's growl died away, he stood with his tail planted firmly between his legs. His eyes were fixed solidly on the window, as were Mark's. Then Titus howled. A howl such as I've never heard before—stark terror emerged in thick, penetrating waves, flecks of spittle dripped from his mouth.

"There!" Mark's cry cut harshly through Titus's anguished yelp. "See him?"

My gaze followed the pointing finger. Then turned to Mark in amazement. What on earth was he talking about? "See who, Mark? There's no one there."

He leaped up and started towards the window then suddenly stopped, as if he smashed into an invisible brick wall. At that same instant a blast of icy air hit me hard across the face and a boom reminiscent of a crash of thunder rolling in from the distance assaulted my ears. Mark's jaw dropped. His eyes widened. He yelled—a yell of tremendous pain. He spun round, hands clasped to his ears, his face contorted by agony.

Titus was still howling. As his howl died away so did the distant thunderclap, leaving silence to reign once more. Mark's face gradually uncreased.

"It's gone," he breathed, glancing from one to the other of us in bewilderment. "What was it?"

All I could do was shake my head.

"Didn't you see him?" he pleaded. "Simon, Bob, Helen? Didn't any of you see him?"

Dad's voice gave nothing away. "See who, Mark?" he asked gently.

"The face at the window."

I feigned ignorance. "I saw a shadow flit past. Probably a cloud, that's all."

He let out an exasperated yell. "No. That man was there again looking in at us. Then he shouted through the window."

My head felt frozen in a block of ice. Swiftly, like wildfire, the ice dropped to my shoulders, causing them to twitch noticeably before the feeling slid down my back.

I looked at Dad. *What can we do?* I screamed at him silently. *What can we do about this?*

"Tell us what you saw, Mark," said Dad gently. "Exactly what you saw and heard."

Mark looked at us all in turn. "But you must have seen and heard him too. He was plain enough. And loud enough."

"I saw his silhouette, that's all." Dad's voice was tranquillity itself. "From the angle we were sitting we could probably only see his shadow. It seems you were the only one who saw him clearly."

"But when he spoke? When he shouted at me?"

"All I heard was thunder," I said. "His words must have been drowned out by that. What did he say?"

Given a different set of circumstances, the dumbstruck look on Mark's face would have been comical. As it was, it froze me to the very core, and his next words did nothing to help matters.

"Thunder?" he said. "I didn't hear any thunder. Only that dreadful screaming voice."

"From the beginning, Mark." Dad said again, his voice gentle, persuasive, "What did you see? What did you hear?"

"It was just after Titus started whining. A man walked past the window. Then suddenly he was back, out of the shadows and in clear view. He pressed his face up to the glass and looked in at us. He looked all around until he saw me. Then he gave a—how can I describe it? A sort of leering glare. As I jumped up I felt a wind blow, but it came from the closed window, and it was so cold."

That last part, about the wind, fitted perfectly with what I experienced. But it was the only bit that did.

"Then he screamed at me, hurting my ears. And yet. . ." He broke off, staring blindly at the wall.

"Go on, Mark," Dad prompted again.

"Although I heard his words clearly enough, just as if he were in the room with us, his lips didn't move at all!" His voice was rising in pitch as he spoke. He looked wildly across at me. "I didn't realise that until now. But they definitely didn't move. He spoke to me, but his lips didn't move. I'm not going crazy, am I?"

Helen cut in. "As Simon said, all we heard was thunder, and all we saw was a quick movement past the window. But no, that doesn't mean you're going mad. Not after everything that's been happening here over the last few days."

"Helen. No more." But even before I spoke I knew it was too late. She had let the cat out of the bag. Anyway, Mark's experience could probably tell us a lot.

"What did he say to you, Mark?" Dad was determined to know the truth.

Mark shivered. "He shouted my name. Said I had no place here and to leave his property alone."

"His property?" mused Dad. "Were those his exact words?"

Mark forced a smile as he bobbed down to greet Titus who was gingerly nuzzling his hand. "He yelled, 'Leave alone that which is mine,' and that was it. He simply disappeared then."

Dad made a snap decision but one that I am convinced was right. "I think we owe you something of an explanation," he said. "At least it's as much of an explanation as we've got at the moment. But after what you've just seen and heard you're entitled to know what we all know."

And so we unfolded our story to Helen's boyfriend, who listened without a word until we finished. Finally, he leaned back in his chair and laughed nervously.

"Well, I must say it would seem to be a simple and easy explanation."

"For goodness' sake," snapped Helen. "How can you sit there and calmly say a ghost is simple and easy?"

"If I hadn't seen that face and heard the voice I probably wouldn't even consider it," Mark told her gently. "But I did see it and I did hear it. There was something outside tonight that just doesn't add up. When you look at what's happened over the last few days you must admit that the theory fits the facts, however improbable it seems. It was Sherlock Holmes who used to say that, wasn't it?"

Every eye in the room was on Mark while he contemplated our story. "Normally I'd insist there must be some rational explanation," he said. "And there probably is, but. . ."

The ticking of the clock was the only discernible sound in the room. I could imagine what he was going through because, no doubt, it was the same sensation I felt a few days earlier. The moment the realisation dawned on me that what was going on was totally beyond the normal realms of reason had been a weird one, to say the least. At first I didn't want to believe it because it seemed so unreasonable and stupid, but when everything was taken into account it was, as Mark succinctly put it, the only theory which fitted the facts.

"It's that face," he continued, "talking to me without moving its lips."

Later that night, just as I was on the verge of drifting into a troubled sleep, Helen tiptoed into my room. She knelt by my bed looking small and vulnerable. "I'm scared, Simon. So scared," she whispered. "What's going on?"

I ran my finger gently down her hair. "I just don't know." What more could I say?

* * *

It must have been a furious storm. I could hear it roaring in the distance, hurtling ever nearer. I knew I was lost and had stopped running—only then realising that I had been running at all. I had no idea where I was, where I was going, or where I'd been. And the noise was getting closer, angrier, louder, all the time.

Suddenly I was cognizant that something was battering my bedroom window. But I wasn't in my bedroom. How could I be when I'd been running so fast? But—yes, that was it—the noise was a storm outside. It was the wind whistling through the trees and the rain hammering on the glass.

But then it was clear that I wasn't in my bedroom after all. I was outside on the lawn looking up at the house. It wasn't raining, but I could still feel the wind whistling above me, an evil, icy blast, and I knew I had to get away from it. I started to run towards the house.

In a few short bounds, I was at the dining room window looking inside. Mum and Dad, Sarah and Helen, were all sitting at the table. Helen turned towards me, and I did my best not to cry out. It was only Helen's face by proxy. The features were hers alright, but as I looked at her they started to twist and mould into something new, something unspeakable and evil.

Suddenly I was sitting alongside her in the dining room and we were both staring at the window. Helen reached out and gripped my shoulder. The shape was outside again, just for a fraction of a second. The noise of the storm boomed on, that interminable whistling coming ever closer.

I turned to comfort Helen; her neck felt cold and bony. My fingers closed around a skeleton. A gleaming, grinning skull with empty eye sockets turned to face me. I pushed the foul thing away, retching from the deep pit of my stomach, knocking my chair over in my haste to get away from it. As I reached the door I realised it wasn't the door at all, but the window through which I could see Helen running across the lawn, her bare feet flying over the grass. And she was not alone. A dark shape hovered menacingly above the trees.

The whistling had become overpowering, and I clamped my hands tightly over my ears. One second it was there, vicious and intense. The next second it was replaced by a muffled roar, and I was flung through the air. I crashed to the ground with a sickening thud and rolled over quickly.

I was in bed sitting bolt upright, heart pounding wildly. I looked uneasily around the room. My hair and forehead were damp with sweat. The dream, which just a few seconds ago had seemed so real, was rapidly fading into memory. Before I flopped down heavily on the pillow and attempted to will sleep to come back, I glanced at the clock. Quarter past four.

*   *   *

The sound of raised voices floated up to my bedroom as I opened the door the next morning and became clearer as I moved along the landing and downstairs.

"You really should, Helen," Mark was saying. I strained to hear his voice, the softer of the two. I didn't need to strain, however, to hear Helen's response.

"No, I don't want to talk about it. Remembering anything about it only makes it worse. Whatever it is, it hasn't harmed us, has it?"

Mark's response was indistinct but I could imagine him trying to soothe her and pictured his arm around her shoulders, squeezing her to him.

I started whistling, not wishing to interrupt anything unannounced. Their conversation stopped abruptly, and as I opened the kitchen door I felt about as wanted as a blackbird at the worms' annual ball.

"Morning," I said, cheerfully, trying not to notice the telltale red rings around my sister's eyes. She smiled up at me from the breakfast table. Mark's arm was indeed around her. Her eyes shone brightly through the hint of tears.

Mark ploughed straight in. "Simon, I'm trying to persuade Helen that we should do something about this. You can't carry on as if nothing's happening."

Instantly I went on the defensive. "I think that's our problem, not yours." I felt I could do no better than echo Helen's feelings. "Besides it isn't as if it's done anything to hurt us."

"Anything that affects Helen affects me." Mark was using an old cliché, but it certainly rang true.

"Yes," I retorted, "but looking at it logically, there's nothing we can do at the moment. We don't know what it is. We don't know what it wants."

"Looking at it logically"—his tone was a reservoir of sarcasm—"the only conclusion we can draw is that it definitely wants *something,* and we must find out what."

I could see he had been analysing the problem properly. "Okay, go on," I urged.

"Right. It's only just started appearing to you, hasn't it?"

My nod was sufficient answer.

"So there must be something it wants now. What we have to ask ourselves is what and why now? I saw a face at the window and I heard it speak. You didn't. It spoke directly to me, even called my name. So logically it affects me every bit as much as you. If you'd seen that face, heard that awful voice. . ." His words trailed away, as no doubt he was painfully reliving his experiences of the previous night.

Helen clamped her hand on top of his, which still rested protectively on her right shoulder. "But if we leave it alone won't it go away?" she asked.

Mark's answer opened another train of thought. "If you want something badly enough you don't give up until you've got it, do you?"

"Not unless I knew it was impossible to get," I admitted.

"But you don't know it's impossible until you've tried everything in your power. What makes you think your visitor will be any different?" Mark asked.

Tears welled up in her eyes again before she buried her head in Mark's chest. "What are we going to do?" she sobbed.

Mark looked across at me as he gently stroked Helen's hair. Then he slowly eased her face away from his dressing gown. "You pop up and get dressed," he murmured to her softly. "We'll go for a walk. It's a lovely day out there."

I suspected he had asked her to leave for a purpose and I closed the door quietly behind her.

"I take it Mum's gone out already," I said, "or Helen wouldn't be acting like that."

"Some committee or other. I forget what she said."

"Helen's been trying to put a brave face on all this but it's starting to get to her. I think we're all a little on edge and mystified by what's going on, but we're managing to take it in our stride. It's hitting Helen hard, though."

"That's why I suggested she get dressed. I want to talk to you."

I smiled. "I thought so."

"Is there any history to this house?" asked Mark. "Anything at all that might explain why this is happening?"

"What do you mean. . . history?"

"Oh, I don't know. Things like they find in horror movies and ghost stories. Was anyone murdered here, or die in any other unnatural way? They do say that houses can sometimes retain a sort of electrical energy over the years and play back events from the past."

"There is something, I think." I tried to recall what I overheard Mum and Dad talking about not long after we moved in four years ago. "But it wasn't anything particularly sinister. I think someone died here during the war."

"How old's the house?"

"It was built in 1930."

Mark nodded slowly and I could sense his keen analytic mind going into a higher gear. "Presumably, in a village like this there are lots of old folk who've lived here most of their lives?"

I began to follow his train of thought, but before I could say anything he was in full swing. "They'll know if anything's happened here and whether there's any village gossip about the place."

"The former postmistress may be able to help us. Ms. Riley's lived here for goodness knows how long. She retired a few months after we moved in, and her father ran the shop before her. If anyone knows anything, I'll bet it's her."

"Good." Mark rubbed his hands together briskly. "We'll know where you are then if we need you."

I sometimes wondered if I lacked anything in the way of common sense. "I don't follow you."

"You'll be with old Mother Riley."

"Aren't we all going to see her?"

Mark shook his head. "No. The way Helen's behaving I think it's best if we keep her well away from anything that might upset her. To hear someone talking about it would probably start it all off again. I'll take her down to the river while you pop over to see Ms. Riley."

CHAPTER 6: DISCOVERY

WHAT ON EARTH was I to say to the old crone? I tried to formulate my opening gambit as I made my way across the village green towards her picturesque thatched cottage. Ms. Riley was, as Dad put it, of the old school. Apparently she always said she wanted to carry on at the shop until her dying day. But in the end her rheumatoid arthritis made it impossible for her to keep going.

Her white latticed gate squeaked as I pushed it open, and I noticed one of the hinges was virtually eaten away by rust. While the gate may have been neglected, the garden itself certainly was not, and I recalled the number of times I had walked past and saw her shuffling about painfully with a trowel and bedding plants. The rolled cinder path ran straight to the green front door, which was embellished with a climbing rose. The fragrance of some early flowering plants wafted towards me and a mass of bright red petals flamed like a beacon against the grape vine on the cottage wall.

For a moment I stood transfixed halfway along the path, completely awed that the beauty around me was created by a frail old woman. As my eyes drifted around the garden, I caught sight of the old woman's face peering suspiciously out at me from behind a scrupulously clean net curtain.

Once she recognized me the suspicion faded almost at once, and her face transformed with a simple smile. Her old gnarled hand came into view and a twisted finger pointed towards the door. "Come in, Simon," she called. Age had done nothing to weary the plummy accent, except perhaps to make it a trifle more cracked and unsteady than I remembered it.

It seemed an eternity from the time her face disappeared to the when the door was pulled open. "How lovely to see you," she said.

"I don't get too many visitors nowadays. People can't be bothered with an old woman like me."

I smiled as I stepped slowly into the past. At least, that was what it felt like when I crossed the threshold. The three sounds that hit me straight away could have been suspended there in that house since the turn of the century: the slow rhythmic tick of the grandfather clock halfway down the narrow, dim, hallway; the uneven heavy breathing coming from the old woman ahead of me; and the swish of her slippers as she shuffled along. The nineteenth-century illusion was complete when she led the way into her tiny lounge. The Old Curiosity Shop had nothing on this place. The room was packed with relics of a bygone age: an oval mahogany table deeply pitted and scarred by the passage of time, a hideously carved bureau with protruding bulbous handles at regular intervals interspersed with heavy brass pullers, a Victorian suite of furniture complete with crocheted antimacassars, and two padded footstools, one of which was now adequately occupied by a huge ginger cat.

Everywhere I looked there were faded black and white photographs in ornate gilt frames. The pictures were all of people, mostly head and shoulders; only occasionally had the photographer opted for a full-length shot.

The only concession to the present-day 1980s was a two-tone grey telephone that looked starkly out of place on an antique table next to the settee.

"Do sit down," croaked the old voice. "I don't have any beer in the house, but perhaps you'll have some sherry. I do keep a nice drop of dry sherry in."

"No thanks, Ms. Riley. It's a little too early for me. But I would like a chat with you."

The rheumy eyes made a passable attempt at gleaming. "A chat. How lovely. I don't get out much nowadays and I do love a good chat. I really miss seeing people at my little shop, you know."

I stood hesitantly by the chair she indicated for me, waiting for her to sit first.

"You sit down there," she insisted. "I'll go and make us a nice cup of tea. It's not too early for that is it, dearie?" She chuckled as if she had made a joke, and headed painfully towards the door.

As far as I was concerned, it was always too early for tea. I hated the stuff. "Tea'll be fine," I lied, hoping my face wouldn't give me away.

The cluttered room pressed claustrophobically around me, forcing me to breathe air from a past generation. A large presentation clock on the mantelpiece ticked its life away, and its hands traversed eight minutes before I heard Ms. Riley's slippers shuffling towards me on the hall carpet. She pushed the door open and inched her way towards a single-legged piecrust table alongside my chair.

"Move that magazine off the table," she said. Her hands shook, rattling the pot and teacups sitting on the flowered tray.

Once her glossy copy of *Home and Country* was safely deposited onto the floor, I took one of the steaming bone china cups and saucers and placed it squarely in the centre of the table, then I jumped up and moved the telephone, making room for the tray on the larger table near the settee.

"Thank you, dearie." She sighed as she lowered herself gingerly on to the seat. "This is nice of you, Simon. I do love having a chat. Most youngsters wouldn't dream of coming round to see me."

I smiled indulgently, wondering how I could possibly tell her I hadn't come out of the goodness of my heart.

"Ms. Riley, I wonder if—?"

"How's your dear mother? I haven't seen her for a couple of weeks. Is she keeping well?"

"Er, yes. She's fine, thanks. She does a lot of visiting nowadays. Official visiting, that is. Hospitals and the prison."

"Yes, I remember when she tried to get me to go prison-visiting. In those days, of course, I couldn't leave the shop. Now I'm retired with time to do all these things, and my health just isn't up to it. Arthritis, you know."

"Yes, it must be difficult for you. Ms. Riley, it's about our house—"

"And your Father, how's he keeping? He had a touch of pleurisy last year, didn't he? Has he fully recovered? Pleurisy can be a nasty business. Painful, as well."

"Yes, he's better now. Do you know anything about the history of—?"

"Oh good. I had pleurisy twice a few years ago. Confined to my bed for weeks, I was, the first time. It didn't hit me quite so hard the second time but every breath still felt like I was being stabbed."

I gave up, deciding to wait until she finished.

"Didn't I read in the paper that he was promoted recently?" she asked.

"Yes, about six months ago. He's the chief environmental health officer for the whole district now."

She beamed. "I'm so glad. I like your father. He's a good man. He was always so polite when he came into the shop. I do miss meeting people over my little counter, you know. It's so kind of you to come and visit an old woman like me."

She paused, taking a sip of tea. The faraway look in her eyes told me she was working something out. "See," she said, "you're eighteen now, aren't you? You must be in the middle of your A levels?"

"I've just finished them. I'm taking things easy at the moment, relaxing, waiting for the results."

She nodded, sipping again.

"Ms. Riley," I ventured, "I was wondering if you could tell me anything about the history of our house?"

"Your house? Whatever for?" It seemed her eyes darted away from mine a little too quickly.

I feigned a certain amount of ignorance with a white lie. "Someone's been telling my sisters tales about it. I want to know the truth so I can hopefully put their minds at rest."

"What sort of stories?" Her question sounded cautious.

"Oh, horror stories and the like. They say it's haunted. Something to do with someone dying there."

The old eyes bored into mine as if trying to probe the real reason for my curiosity. "What's been happening there?"

I shook my head. "Nothing really. It's just that Helen and Sarah have both been told that before we bought White Pastures it was supposed to be haunted."

"Has anything happened?" she persisted.

I hated lying to her, but looking at everything in the cold, hard light of day, it did seem just a little ridiculous.

"No, nothing's happened," I laughed. "But I would like to put their minds at rest. I thought if anyone would know something about the house it would be you. You've lived in the village all your life, haven't you?"

She nodded slowly. "I have, indeed. So's my stepbrother. Why don't you go and see him? He may be able to help."

"The vicar? Does he know anything?"

"He knows more about the village than I do. I'm sure if there's any history to your house he'll be able to tell you."

I sensed I was getting somewhere. "Ms. Riley," I said gently, "it sounds as if there's something I should know."

"I only know what happened during the war. A young woman was killed at your house, but I don't know anything about it being haunted."

She took another sip of tea and stared beyond me out of the window. Sensing that her mind was pushing back the pages of time I waited silently for her to continue. "It was a terrible tragedy," she said eventually. "She was only twenty."

Again there was an uncomfortable silence broken only by the ticking of the mantelpiece clock.

"Go on, Ms. Riley," I urged.

"No one really knew her. She was James Roberts's bride. They'd only just got married when it happened."

"When what happened?" I wished I did not have to continue prompting her.

Her eyes seemed to fix on a spot in deep space—or somewhere around forty years ago.

"The poor boy's mother went out of her mind after it happened. She had to be taken away, you know. It was awful."

This was beginning to get rather exasperating. "Ms. Riley, what *did* happen?"

"During the war James Roberts had a reserved occupation." She caught my puzzled look. "It meant he wasn't called up to serve in the armed forces. Something to do with the railway, I think. Anyway, he said he couldn't stay at home doing nothing for the war effort with the Nazis getting closer to our doorstep all the time, so he enlisted. If he hadn't, he wouldn't have met her and it would never have happened."

I hoped this was leading somewhere, to something I wanted to know.

She returned her gaze to that same distant spot and launched into her tale. "The Roberts were mainly a banking family, and it came as a great disappointment to old man Neville Roberts that his only son wasn't interested in the bank. They lived in a big house between here and Westdean." Ms. Riley turned to look at me. "Hollycourt Grange. Where Colonel Barratt lives now."

"I know it," I answered encouragingly.

"The old man partly got his way in that young James did study figures—accountancy—but that was all. He was adamant that he wasn't going into the bank. Instead he joined the railways in town. Quite a good job he got, and I think it appeased his father a little. Anyway, the war came along and James joined up. It wasn't long before he was an officer. One time when he came home on leave, he brought a girl with him. I forget her name, but my stepbrother will know it." Now that Ms. Riley was well into her story her voice seemed to find new life, sounding more powerful and vibrant than I ever remembered it.

"He said he was going to marry her, which was another shock for old man Neville, but I think he finally realised he'd lose his son if he didn't agree to it. So he bought White Pastures for them as a kind of peace offering. That was the talk of the village, I can tell you, a big house like that with all its grounds just for the two of them. It's a fine family home, as you well know, of course, but I think a lot of folk round here felt it was too good for a young married couple.

"Then it happened. James got a few weeks' leave and they were married here in the village. A week later his young bride was dead and he disappeared."

"He killed her?" I asked incredulously.

Ms. Riley shook her head fiercely. "No, nothing like that. It was during a German bombing raid in the middle of the night. We don't know whether the Germans lost their way or whether it was intentional, but Meriton was bombed. There was a lot of damage in the village and one bomb hit White Pastures' gardens. That's what killed her."

My heart was thumping. Our house was bombed during the war!

She turned to gaze into space again. "For some reason the young couple were outside when the bomb fell and the girl was killed. I remember seeing James at the funeral. He was heartbroken. And that was the last anyone saw of him. He set off from the church to go back to White Pastures and was never seen again."

It was like something out of a weepy 1950s film. *What an amazing story*, I thought.

"And there've been no reports of any ghosts or anything?" I asked rather slowly.

Again the old head shook in silent answer. It was a good half minute before she dragged her gaze back to my face. "No, nothing like that. Not that's reached my ears, anyway. I was very friendly with the Hammonds, who owned White Pastures before you, and they never mentioned anything about ghosts."

Well, what do I have? I wondered as I made my way back across the village green. I had an interesting snippet of information about the house's history, but it all happened more than forty years ago. Could it be connected to the events of the last few days?

CHAPTER 7: THE VICAR

MUM WAS STILL at her committee meeting when I got home so I looked in the fridge for some lunch. Halfway through my cold roast beef, lettuce, cucumber, and tomatoes, Helen and Mark returned from their walk by the river.

Helen scuttled upstairs to change into her bikini while Mark sat across the table from me astride his chair. "Did you find anything?" he asked.

"I found out a little bit about the house." I recounted what Ms. Riley had told me.

Mark raised his eyebrows. "And what did the vicar have to say?"

"Give me a chance," I protested. "I've not been to see him yet."

"Well, that's your afternoon sorted out," Mark said in that brisk manner of his. "I'll keep Helen company here, sunbathing."

"Now look. . ." I started to say, becoming a little irritated that he seemed to be taking over. But I realised he was probably right, and I was just as anxious to get to the bottom of the situation as he was. After all, it was my sister who was suffering. "Okay, I'll pop over to the vicarage straight after lunch."

"You say the old woman was a bit reluctant at first?" Mark leaned back on the chair.

"Only when I first asked about the house. It was almost as if she expected something was happening here." I recalled the slight frown that creased her forehead when I finally succeeded in steering her to the subject, and the way her eyes indicated that she may have been remembering something.

"Could she know more than she's letting on?" asked Mark.

"Could be. But why shouldn't she tell us the truth?"

He shrugged. "I don't know. Let's see what this vicar's got to say, anyway. What's he like?"

"I don't really know him. Mum often talks about him, though. She bumps into him on committees and things, but we don't go to church. I've seen him around on his bike, but that's about all."

"If he's Ms. Riley's stepbrother he'll be quite old, won't he?"

"He is. Early seventies I suppose. I remember reading a feature about him in the local paper a few months ago. I think it said that several years ago he had to apply to the church authorities to be allowed to stay on here past his normal retirement age."

Mark smiled. "I wonder what they do with retired vicars? Probably put them out to pasture to tend sheep of a different flock."

*   *   *

The church and its vicarage shared a common drive that divided into two, the church to the left and the house to the right. The vicarage was a large building with two leaded casement windows on either side of an ancient oak door badly in need of fresh paint. The old bricks were chipped and had a coat of moss in places where damp seemed to have crept in. The mortar between them was loose and flaky, looking as if it could be pried out with a feather. The wooden window frames were so rotten I was surprised the glass had not fallen out long ago.

The doorbell was like an old-fashioned clock key, which I had to turn a couple of times before its summons rang throughout the house. While I waited, I imagined slow, solid footsteps making their way to the door from the dark depths of the interior. The bolt on the door would be drawn back, creaking for want of oil, and the old, rusty hinges would squeal in protest as the door eased aside to reveal a tall, bald servant—possibly cross-eyed—who would boom out just one word in a deep, hollow voice: "Yes?"

Hearing that one word snapped me back to reality. The voice that gave it life was sturdy and strong but in no way belonged to a tall, bald servant. My imagined scene disappeared as I found myself looking upon a small, stocky woman wearing a flowered apron over a light checked dress. Her grey eyes matched her hair, which was drawn up tightly across her scalp and fastened into a bun.

"Is the Reverend McBeil in, please?" I asked.

Her severe face broke into a smile. "Yes, he is. Won't you come in?" She stepped aside and I walked through into an aroma of freshly baked bread. Then I noticed her hands were marked with flour.

"I'm sorry," I said. "Have I disturbed your baking?"

I guessed she was probably lying when she shook her head. "No, not really. I'd just put a couple of loaves in the oven and was about to start clearing up. I'll tell the vicar you're here." She looked me up and down. "Who shall I say's calling? We haven't seen you here before, have we?"

Here I was, feeling guilty about never having stepped inside the man's church before I even met him. I suppose my weak smile was reminiscent of Sarah's sheepish grin when she was caught out.

"No, er, I'm afraid I'm usually busy on Sundays. Revising, you know. A levels."

She nodded knowingly.

"Simon Reynolds," I told her.

"If you'll come this way I'll let the vicar know."

The strip of carpeting that ran down the middle of the dimly lit passage was threadbare in many places and had frayed, tattered edges. My guide tapped on a closed door a couple of times and waited for a muffled "come in" before opening it.

"Mr. Simon Reynolds to see you, sir," she said, ushering me inside. As soon as I was over the threshold, she stepped back out, shutting the door as she went.

For a second I felt like the fly who walked into the spider's parlour. But this was no parlour, and the man who sat writing at the battered mahogany desk by the window was no spider. He pushed back his chair and stood to greet me. The Reverend Hubert McBeil just about matched my own height of five feet eleven, and my earlier estimate of his age looked to be just about right. A thick mane of pure white hair was parted on the right and a couple of locks reached down towards his equally white left eyebrow. He had a kindly face with a few laugh lines just visible behind his dark-rimmed glasses.

"You're Jean Reynolds's lad, aren't you?" he asked, extending his arm. The handshake was firm; he squeezed my fingers painfully into each other.

"That's right. I was hoping you'd be able to help me." I never did believe in beating about the bush, preferring instead to plunge straight in.

"Of course, young man, if I can. Come and sit down. I'll get Mrs. Jackson to bring us some tea."

Tea again! I had managed to leave half a cup of the foul stuff at his stepsister's cottage, but I got the distinct impression that his piercing, blue eyes sitting atop his fleshy, rounded nose would notice if I tried it here. He pressed a button on the corner of his desk, which I imagined rang a summons in the kitchen just as Mrs. Jackson had plunged her hands into flour again. I smiled as my mind's eye saw her tutting impatiently, reaching for the towel.

The room was obviously the vicar's study. A couple of bookcases lined one wall and a closed bureau stood by the door. His cluttered desk indicated he was starting to prepare his sermon for the upcoming Sunday. We sat at a small wooden table in the centre of the room on which the obligatory bone china teacups were housed, accompanied by one of the lightest, most delicious sponge cakes I had ever tasted, probably the result of one of Mrs. Jackson's earlier forays into the world of baking.

"Now then, my boy, what's troubling you?"

I hadn't really thought where to begin. "Your stepsister suggested I should see you. She thought you may be able to throw some light on a few strange things that've been happening at our house lately."

He looked up sharply. "Did she now? And what made her say that?"

"I went to see her to ask if—" I broke off suddenly. Damn! My little white lie to Ms. Riley was undone. I told her nothing had happened, that I merely wanted to put my sisters' minds at rest, now here I was blurting out the whole truth to the vicar.

His eyes bored into mine, presumably because he was wondering about my hesitation. Well, there was no backing out now. "I'm afraid I didn't tell Ms. Riley the full truth," I said, no doubt looking a little shamefaced as he raised his eyebrows. "I didn't want to worry her unnecessarily, but I feel it would be better if you knew the whole story."

Silently he waited for me to continue. I tried to give him as many details as possible, leaving nothing out, from that first glimpse of a dark shadow flitting past the window to Mark's experience of the previous night. I also told him what Ms. Riley said about the house being bombed during the war.

"That was a terrible business," he said. "Poor Heidi being killed by that bomb. And her husband. . . " He seemed to snap out of his reminiscence almost before it started. "But I really have no idea about what's happening now. There's certainly no history of anything unusual that I know of. The Hammonds, who had White Pastures before you, were regular churchgoers and I'm sure they'd have come to me straight away if anything was troubling them."

"Can you tell me a little more about what happened during the war?"

The vicar turned towards the window. He didn't answer for several seconds, and when he looked back at me his eyes seemed distant, as if lost in thought.

"There's not much to tell. I can only reiterate what my stepsister's already told you. Meriton was bombed at the end of the war and young Heidi Roberts was killed. Jim, her husband, said she was terrified during air raids but always refused to go down to their air raid shelter, fearing they'd be buried alive." His words came slowly, creating the impression he was choosing them carefully. "That night was the closest they'd ever been to an actual bombing and Jim said the noise of the aircraft and the bombs falling nearby had terrified her beyond all reason. She fled into the garden and he was chasing her when the Germans scored a direct hit. Heidi was killed instantly."

"And. . .?"

He leaned back, avoiding my eyes as he turned to the window again. "There really is no more to tell."

I glanced down at my teacup, which was still more than three-quarters full. "I'm grateful you've told me this," I said, even though there was nothing new in it. It was just a rehash of what I learned earlier. "Many thanks."

He nodded silently as I stood up.

"I'll be off, then. Thank you again," I said.

The vicar looked at me thoughtfully. "Would you like me to come to the house to see if I think there is a spirit there?"

"I don't think so, not yet. It would probably only frighten the girls even more. Can we leave it for a while and if it gets worse I'll let you know? Maybe you could come then."

"Whenever you want me, Simon. You know I'll be there for you."

"And I'd be grateful if you didn't mention this to my mother."

"If that's what you want," he murmured as I walked towards the door.

"Oh, Simon," he called suddenly. "Don't forget your tea."

CHAPTER 8: FIRST ATTACKS

WHEN I ARRIVED HOME, Sarah was back from school and had joined Mark and Helen who were sunbathing on the lawn. Titus was lying in the shade of the trees at the edge of the grass and wearily raised his head when I came out through the patio door. His tail wagged briefly as I stopped to pat him, and within seconds he was asleep again. Although Mark must have been dying to ask what the vicar said, he merely waved a tanned arm.

"Hi," he called cheerily.

"I can't understand why you'd rather be at a friend's house talking about computers all afternoon when you could be out here," Helen said. So that's how he'd explained my absence to Helen.

"It was worth it," I fired back, "He showed me a couple of short cuts for programming my new multimedia computer. Do you want to see?"

"Sure." Mark heaved himself up and we went indoors together.

"That was a waste of time," I said when we were alone in my room. "He doesn't know any more than Ms. Riley. He says he'll come over sometime if we want him to, though, to see if there's anything here."

"A good idea, but not when Helen's around."

"That's what I thought. We'll see what happens over the next few days."

Mark sat down at my Amstrad Multimedia PC and switched it on. "This is some machine," he enthused, his fingers flashing deftly across the 83-key layout, watching, obviously impressed, as a program I had set up for my modern history revision flashed on to the Super VGA monitor.

"Glad you like it. You're playing with nearly £2,000 worth of hardware there."

"Have you got any games for it?"

"Not for this one. This is what I call my professional machine. I've got plenty for the Commodore, though."

"You've got two computers?"

"Yeah, I had the Commodore a few years ago, to practice on and get used to computers, then Dad got me this one for more serious use. Can you get the Commodore out—it's in that cupboard—and set it up, please. Connect it to the telly. I'll get some games."

As I rummaged through my immense collection of software, my fingers closed around one particular game disc.

"I think you'll like this one," I smiled as I pulled it out.

Mark withdrew his head from the cupboard and grinned when I revealed its title: *Ghostbusters*.

"I've got to go to the loo," I said, putting the disc on to the workstation. "It's all this tea that's been forced down me today. Can you load it, please? I'll be back in a sec."

When I returned a couple of moments later Mark was looking decidedly puzzled.

"This *Ghostbusters* is a funny program, isn't it? I can't make head nor tail of it."

"What? It's simple enough." Peering over his shoulder at the screen, my face must have reflected Mark's astonishment.

"That's not right," I muttered, staring at the words shining back at me. "How long's it been saying that?"

"I put the disc in, which loaded okay. Then it started searching and came up with this. I've played *Ghostbusters* before, but it wasn't like this."

The words took up just one line on the screen: "Ghost hunters searching. What for?"

I went to press the reset button, but Mark gripped my arm. "No, that's not all. Wait a moment. Watch what happens next. I've been through this cycle three times now."

Almost as he spoke, the screen went blank before another line flashed on it: "Ghosts also hunting. Ghost hunters can't help. Leave alone."

"What the fuck's this?" I said. "I've never seen this before."

Had a computer been capable of anger, I would say my Commodore achieved it in the next few seconds. Words hurtled across the screen. At first there was no meaning to them, just letters and words appearing in a nonsensical, tangled jumble. But eventually the superfluous whisked into oblivion, leaving one stark message: "No danger if left. Great danger to meddle. Heed warning. Don't mock."

I looked at Mark, suspicions forming. "What have you done?" I demanded. Turning my attention to the drive system my finger poised above the eject button, I expected him to stop me. He didn't.

"You've put this program in," I continued angrily. "If you've wiped my *Ghostbusters*—"

"I haven't done anything. I loaded the disc and this is what happened."

The screen cleared again ahead of the green lettering, flashing up its earlier message: "Ghost hunters searching. What for?"

Mark's eyes shone as he turned to me. "It's asking us a question. Why don't we answer it?"

"What? Who's asking us a question, for fuck's sake? This isn't on the program."

"Someone's asking. You can't get away from that, can you?" He pointed to the screen.

That was true enough; the words were there before my eyes. "Go on, then," I nodded. "What shall we tell it?"

Mark keyed in his answer beneath the question: "Ghosts."

That disappeared in seconds, replaced by another query: "Ghost hunters search for ghosts. Where?"

I could hardly believe this was happening. "Are you sure the disc's in the right way. This couldn't somehow be the other side. . .Could it?" My voice trailed away as I realised how stupid I sounded.

Mark ignored me and keyed in another answer: "White Pastures."

The computer had hardly digested that before flashing up its own response. "Ends."

"Hey, wait a minute," shouted Mark, but to no avail. The screen went blank and no amount of us keying in prompts could get it to respond.

"Load it again and see what happens," I suggested. Mechanically Mark went through the process again, but this time the *Ghostbusters* game program appeared properly. We tried a third time, with the same result.

Mark's face was ashen as he turned to me. "That saves the vicar a trip. We know there's something definitely here now, don't we?"

"Why wouldn't it wait? We could have found out what it wanted."

"What are you going to do about it?"

"How do you mean?"

"Are you going to tell your dad?"

"Dunno. What do you think?"

"I definitely wouldn't tell Helen. I didn't like that warning. What was it? 'Dangerous to meddle'?"

"Yeah, that's what it said. Look, let's keep this to ourselves for now. There's no point worrying the others."

The colour was beginning to return to Mark's cheeks, and I guessed his sense of adventure was making itself felt when he asked me with a half-smile, "What do you say to trying again later?"

"I say fuck yes."

*   *   *

We spent what was left of the afternoon soaking up the sun with Helen and Sarah. The sun kept some of its warmth right up to the time it started to dip behind the trees. Mum's timing couldn't have been better; I had just shivered and decided to go in when she called from the kitchen window, "Dinner in 20 minutes."

Sarah was up in a flash and ran across the lawn towards the patio door.

"Leave that if you like," said Mark as Helen started to shake her towel. "I'll do that."

She grinned at each of us in turn. "Thanks."

Mark's eyes followed her across the grass. He smiled at her as she turned in the doorway to give us a flowery wave. "Straight after dinner, then?"

"I reckon. What do you think we'll—?" I broke off at the sound of Sarah's frantic scream and I whirled round towards the house.

"What the hell's that?" cried Mark, turning his gaze towards Sarah's bedroom window above the dining room patio doors.

Sarah continued to scream hysterically as we flew through the house and upstairs. By the time we reached her room, Helen, Mum, and Dad were already with her, staring in disbelief at the upturned furniture.

The contents of her drawers and wardrobes were strewn haphazardly across the floor.

Dad turned to us, anger flashing. "Did either of you two do this?"

Mark flushed, whether from embarrassment or rage, I couldn't tell at that moment. "Bob, I resent—"

"Mark, if you didn't do it, just say so. Let's not have any of your speeches, I'm not in the mood right now." I'd never heard Dad speak to anyone like that before.

"Of course I didn't do it," snapped Mark. "What do you think—?"

Again Dad cut him short. "Simon, what about you?"

"You don't really think I'd do this, do you?" I felt hurt and angry that he could even think I was capable of wrecking my sister's room. Apple-pie her bed now and again, yes, but nothing like this.

"Somebody did it. And there's no one else in the house."

Even as Dad spoke, an almighty crash came from the other end of the landing in the direction of my room, and Mum and Dad's. For a few seconds we neither moved nor uttered a sound.

Then Dad put a finger to his lips. "Shhh. Careful." He tiptoed out into the passage with Mark and me close behind.

Inch by inch we crept towards the two rooms at that end of the house. The noise definitely came from one of them, and sounded like a wardrobe toppling over. My heart pounded as I suddenly became aware of how heavily I was breathing. I tried to hold my breath, but that only made my heart hammer all the more.

Dad pressed his ear to the closed door of his room and indicated for me to do the same at mine. "When I give the signal," he whispered, "throw your door open."

My fingers hovered half an inch from the handle. I was sweating much more than I was earlier in the heat of the afternoon sun. I rubbed a clammy palm against the back of my other hand and swallowed fiercely.

Dad looked across at me and nodded. "Now," he yelled. Together we flung open our doors.

My room looked like a hurricane had been through it. My bed was on its side, resting against the wall, the curtains were torn from the window and lay draped across the floor, clothes were flung from my wardrobe—a shirt had even been thrown over the light shade.

The keyboard of my Commodore was crushed and twisted, and the portable television I used as its monitor lay upside down on the floor, surrounded by remnants of its shattered screen. The one thing in the room apparently unscathed was the Amstrad, which sat on the desk.

There was no sign of the perpetrator of this damage. Outrage and a certain amount of fear welled up inside me. Then I heard Dad's voice, quiet and defeated. "Look at this," he said, almost inaudibly. He stood on the threshold of his own room, staring inside with Mark alongside him.

The scene was almost a carbon copy of my room. Chaos and destruction intermingled, from the sliding door of my parents' walk-in wardrobe—which appeared to have been wrenched from its runners and thrown across the bed—to the contents of cupboards and drawers scattered everywhere.

At first my feelings were of overpowering strength and determination to inflict revenge on whoever had desecrated our home in this way. Adrenalin coursed through my veins giving me the conviction that, had they been standing in front of me, I would have killed the vandals with my bare hands. But as I stood helplessly surveying the damage, my stomach started to knot and twist, leaving a sick, hollow sensation.

"We'd better check the other rooms." Dad's words were soft and somewhat vague.

Helen's room was untouched, but the fifth bedroom, the one Mark was using, was in a similar state to ours.

Mum had already begun to put Sarah's clothes back in the wardrobe while my sisters sat on the dishevelled bed in a state of shock, comforting each other.

"We ought to get the police here before we tidy up," Dad insisted, taking one of Sarah's dresses from Mum as she was about to replace it on a hanger.

Sarah looked up with sad, red-ringed eyes. "I don't know when this could have happened," she sobbed. "Everything was okay when I came up to change after school."

"Mark and I were in my room a couple of hours ago," I said. "And you've been downstairs ever since, haven't you, Mum?" She nodded silently. And Dad had said everything was normal when he got home from work at about six o'clock. Somehow it seemed to have slipped everyone's minds that we'd heard that tremendous crash just a few moments ago.

"I'm phoning the police straight away," said Dad. "Don't touch anything."

We were halfway downstairs when Titus suddenly howled. Titus! He had run alongside us on the lawn after Sarah screamed, but I'd no idea what happened to him after that. The events of the last few moments had pushed him from my mind.

The door from the dining room to the hall and staircase was open, just as we had left it, as were the patio doors, but there was no sign of him.

"Titus," I called. "Where are you, old fella?"

"Where the devil's he got to?" Dad snapped irritably after a fruitless inspection of the kitchen.

"He wasn't far away when he howled," said Mum. "I thought it came from the bottom of the stairs."

Then again came that long pitiful howl, this time from outside.

"There he is," cried Helen, pointing through the window. Titus was crouched under a bush on the far side of the lawn, staring towards the house. He responded to our calls by getting up slowly and almost reluctantly creeping across the grass to the patio, but it was there that he stubbornly stood his ground, and no amount of coaxing would persuade him to come inside.

Dad was getting angry. "You see to him while I ring the police. Get him in and lock the doors." That was easier said than done. Each time anyone went near him, he bared his teeth and growled a warning at us. It was almost unheard of for Titus to growl. He was one of the best-natured dogs I'd ever known. The rusty red hair along his back was slightly erect and the poor creature was distinctly ill at ease. His eyes were wild and frightened, constantly peering around, but every few seconds he seemed to fix his gaze over my shoulder at something behind me in the dining room.

"Come on," I whispered gently. "There's no one here. They're gone now. Come and see for yourself." I eased my hand towards him, but withdrew it sharply as he shot forward, snapping at me.

"Whatever's the matter with you?" I shouted, but he didn't seem to hear. Instead he was off like a rocket to the bottom of the garden, where he disappeared amongst the mass of shrubs.

"Leave him," said Mum. "He'll come in when he's ready. We'd better lock the doors, though, like your Dad said."

It was the same police officer who had come before. After taking a quick look at the damage, he decided it was a case for CID.

Two plain-clothes officers from the nearby town of Merebrook were with us within an hour. The taller of the two introduced himself as Detective Sergeant Alan Breck, and his partner as Detective Constable Tony Mitchell. Together they took a quick look over the bedrooms before we all went down to the lounge to explain what had happened.

Breck then went back upstairs for a more detailed look at the devastation while Mitchell took statements from everyone. When it was my turn I made no mention of our strange communication with the computer.

Eventually Breck came down and told us to sift through the rooms to see if anything was missing. "I'm afraid you'll find everything's rather dusty," he apologised. "I've been checking for fingerprints. Do you mind if we take your prints as well? It's just so we can compare them with those I've found in the rooms, to eliminate them. Then any that are left over could belong to the intruder."

I felt decidedly guilty while Mitchell pressed each of my inked fingers on to a sheet of white paper.

"Right," said Breck when everyone was done. "We'll have a look round outside and then be off. Can you pop into the station tomorrow with a list of anything that's missing? I'll get it circulated straight away."

"We'd better get Titus in before you go outside," said Mum. "The mood he was in earlier, I wouldn't trust him with strangers."

"Titus?"

"Our dog. He won't come in the house since it happened."

Breck frowned. "I wonder if they've kicked or hit him. Are there any signs of blood on him?"

"I don't know," Dad admitted rather sheepishly. "He hasn't let us get anywhere near him."

"What's he usually like? Is he rather timid?"

"Just the opposite. He's very outgoing and friendly."

"I'd like to look at him, if I may?"

"I'll see if I can get him in," I volunteered. "He might have calmed down by now."

Titus lay just outside the patio doors and ran in as soon as they were open. He seemed completely back to normal, licking my hand as if he were trying to make amends for snapping at me earlier. He was as good as gold while Breck flicked his fingers through the rusty red hair searching for any signs of cuts or lumps.

"No," the detective said after a couple of moments. "They don't appear to have touched him."

Sarah dropped to her knees and pressed the dog's head to her chest. "Thank goodness. I'd hate to think anyone's hurt him." He licked her nose as if in appreciation of her care.

After the police officers left, we set to our task of clearing up. It was true what Detective Sergeant Breck said about fingerprint dust covering everything. Slowly but surely some semblance of order began to return to my bedroom, but the strange thing was that nothing appeared to be missing. Even my vast collection of computer games was present and unharmed. The only lasting damage was a torn curtain, the Commodore, which was a complete write-off, and the TV that I used as its monitor.

Afterwards, when we all gathered downstairs, Dad walked over to Helen and curled his arm around her shoulders. "The only things that seem to be missing from our room," he said gently, "are your birthday presents."

Sarah gasped. "That's all that's gone from my room too. Along with the present Simon got you."

The jewellery box and gold chain! I'd left the necklace in Sarah's room, intending to wrap it later in the week.

Mark started to say something, then broke off, looking at Dad.

"Bob," —he sounded hesitant, unsure of himself—"was your present wrapped?"

"One was. The other wasn't. I only brought it home with me tonight."

Mark turned to Helen. "I'd got you three things. One was only little, just a token really, not worth much in monetary terms, yet that's gone along with the other two. None of them were wrapped and there was nothing to indicate they were meant as presents."

Tears began to roll down Helen's cheek. "What does all this mean? Why would anyone take just my presents?"

"And more to the point, how did they know which things were presents?" asked Mark.

Whether the rooms were ransacked by human agency or otherwise was impossible to tell, but the remainder of the night passed uneventfully. Titus dozed alongside Dad's chair, only looking up at the window once. Instinctively I stiffened. "What is it, old boy?" All of a sudden, everyone seemed tense and alert. Dad was over to the window and had the curtains aside in a matter of seconds.

"I can't see anyone," he said, peering into the night. Titus, who appeared completely unbothered by the fuss his single glance had caused, put his head back down and closed his eyes. Dad returned to his chair and we focused again on the television. I doubt any of us had the faintest idea what we were watching. I know I didn't.

*   *   *

The sun was already hot when I awoke the next morning.

"What are your plans today?" Mum asked as she popped a couple of slices of bread into the toaster for me.

"Dunno. I'm still a little demob happy, I guess. I can't seem to pluck up the energy to do much except sunbathe at the moment. How about you?"

"I've lent my car to Helen. She's gone off for the day with Mark to the coast somewhere, I think. So it means I'm stuck here. I'd planned to put in a shift at the shop in outpatients, but I've had to ask Marjorie Blackwell to step in for me. I thought it'd do Helen good to get away."

My mind wasn't really on what Mum was saying, instead it kept slipping back to the events of the past few days. In particular to last night's damage. "Have we let the police know that only Helen's birthday presents are missing?"

"Dad was going to tell them on his way to the office," she replied. "You know, the more I think about last night, the stranger it seems. Why take only her presents? There was £50 in cash in the same drawer as the blouse we got her, and it was just scattered over the floor. I don't understand it."

"The criminal mind works in strange ways."

"Do you think it was a burglar?" Mum said, averting her eyes.

"Who else could it have been?" I feigned surprise, hoping my acting ability lent a little weight to the puzzled look.

"You know what I mean." She pretended to adjust the switch on the side of the toaster as a ruse to avoid looking at me. "I was just wondering if it could have anything to do with, you know, this figure we've been seeing."

"Do you think it could?"

"Come on, Simon. You know as well as I do. . ."

"But there've been these burglaries in the village for the last month or so," I protested.

"Professional jobs, all of them," countered Mum. "I was only talking to Mrs. Lowther the other day and she said there was very little damage when her house was broken into. The thieves seemed to know exactly what they wanted: money, video recorders, computers, and silverware. Certainly not teenagers' clothes."

Trust Mum to be so intuitive and down-to-earth, even if her viewpoint did lead to something way up in the clouds. There was no doubt in my mind regarding the real answer, and I began to wonder if we may be able to face up to, and indeed solve, our problem if we worked together. Maybe now was the time for everyone to put their cards on the table and acknowledge openly to each other that our visitor was not of the burgling fraternity, but was instead something altogether more sinister and unknown. That was the most unnerving of all—the unknown.

The other development that disturbed me considerably was the fact that it no longer confined its activities to simply passing by the window. It had found a way inside.

"Do you really believe we've got a ghost or something else from the supernatural world?" I asked.

"You and your Dad seem convinced—"

"Only because it's an easy explanation for certain things that have happened," I interrupted. "Such as the face Mark saw at the window, which he said spoke to him without moving its lips, and the figure we've seen in the garden."

"Oh, I don't know what to think." She sounded weary and irritable as she passed me two underdone slices of toast.

I had laid the butter on thickly and was reaching for the Marmite jar when a memory stirred. "I told Dad a couple of days ago that I'd see if the library had anything on the supernatural. I think I'll nip down straight after breakfast."

* * *

Meriton Library was hardly worthy of the name. It comprised a few hundred books in a large wooden hut that resembled the village hall. In fact, it stood next to the village hall and without the faded notice outside, a stranger would be hard-pressed to distinguish between them. Two librarians shared the job on a part-time basis, but even so, it was only open four mornings and two afternoons a week.

Today was Patricia McLaren's turn to run the desk. She was tall and thin with long lanky hair to match her build. She was a friend of Mum's, so I knew her reasonably well.

"We don't get much call for books like that here," she said in reply to my query about tomes on the supernatural, and I thought she sounded a little like she disapproved. Certainly, the welcoming smile disappeared from her gaunt, narrow face as she pointed me in the right direction. "I don't think we've got many."

She was right about that. There were precisely two books, almost in pristine condition, which stood out starkly from the well-thumbed volumes on either side. I pulled them both down and took them to one of three small tables in the centre of the single room. I wasn't sure what I was expecting to find in them or how they would be able to help. It was more of a long shot than anything.

One of them, *The Unexplainable*, attracted me because its title summed up what was happening at White Pastures. The blurb on the book jacket said the author, Jon Stewart, had gained a PhD in experimental parapsychology and carried out extensive research into supernatural phenomena. According to Dr. Stewart, almost everyone has an experience at some time in their life that they put down to being supernatural, but he claimed that after research less than 4 percent remained unexplained.

His book contained several firsthand and eyewitness accounts of a variety of hauntings, none of which seemed in the least bit frightening in a stuffy library on a hot and bright summer's day. But I knew how quickly that could change. Substitute moonlight for the sun and the possibility of ghosts existing leaped a hundredfold.

It seemed that our type of haunting—where several people independently see the same apparition (namely our fleeting figure outside the window) in the same place at the same time—was among the most commonly reported and, to me, that made it all the more credible. My view was reinforced when I went on to read that it was also very rare for an apparition to be repeatedly seen in the same place by different people at different times.

Looking at it from the other side, though, it was clear that Dr. Stewart's research showed that in the majority of so-called hauntings, ghosts could be explained as tricks of the light or hallucinations; people believed they saw something just because the house in which they lived was reputed to be haunted.

Maybe that did sum up our situation. We now believed our home to be infested by ghosts, so were we more susceptible to seeing things that were not there. And, of course, it was only Mark who had seen and heard the face at the window. *But*, my inner voice said, *he had that experience before suspecting that White Pastures was haunted.*

My thoughts turned again to the previous week when Titus chased the fleeing shadow across the lawn and how the shadow suddenly expanded, threatening to engulf me. It was difficult to recall exactly what had happened without exaggerating it, even to myself. All I could say categorically was that something had flitted across the grass and then I thought I saw it start to wash over me. But could it have been a cloud briefly masking the moon, leaving an eerie patchwork of light on the ground? And had my overwrought imagination taken charge and made too much of a couple of leaves blowing along on either side of me, making me believe a foul character from another dimension was about to drop on me?

How could I apply logic to find answers when there was no logic to the problem? I felt I could go round in circles forever, and so I turned my attention to the other book.

This was a much slimmer volume with the unlikely, and I thought rather jokey, title of *Bump in the Night*. But there was nothing jokey about its contents, which, in a straightforward and business-like manner, dealt with life after death, poltergeists, and black magic rituals that conjured up demons from hell. I had seen enough horror movies and read enough trashy novels to have a rough idea of what a poltergeist was: a malicious spirit that created havoc. Now there was an ideal theory as to the cause of the damage in our bedrooms, I thought, as I turned to the relevant chapter.

"Poltergeist," I read, "is a German word which, in accurate translation, describes this particular type of inexplicable physical manifestation perfectly: noisy spirit. It is associated with a haunting over a period of time and involves, without any visible means, the movement of objects about the house, usually ornaments and crockery, accompanied by strange and frightening noises.

"Sometimes, but by no means always, poltergeists are violent and instead of merely moving objects calmly, will throw them with considerable force. Indeed, thousands of pounds worth of damage can be caused by a poltergeist in less than a minute.

"Poltergeist manifestation, or Spuk as they are also known, have been chronicled for nearly 1,500 years, although actual records of those early cases are extremely rare.

"Their type of haunting is the same today as it has always been; sudden inexplicable bursts of energy affecting inanimate objects. Another factor has been common to almost every known case down the centuries, from those very early ones which man witnessed with eyes and ears only, right up to those monitored by today's sophisticated electronic cameras, audio recorders, vibration detectors and thermometers, and that is that the manifestations appear to revolve around just one person.

"Research has shown that up to the start of the twentieth century the average age of a person at the centre of a poltergeist haunting was sixteen. This has been steadily climbing and now stands at twenty."

I raised my eyes from the page. Everything we were experiencing seemed to suggest a poltergeist. I was eighteen, it was Helen's twentieth birthday in a few days, and someone or something had scattered our clothes and bedroom furniture about. Could Helen be the focus of a poltergeist? Could it even be me? If so, what was causing it?

Eagerly, I read on.

"A lot more work is necessary before we can even begin to scratch the surface of this particularly distressing and frightening form of supernatural phenomenon, but one theory which is proving to be a firm favourite is that the focus person themselves could be the cause, however unwittingly, in that the power to move objects is generated from the person's own mind. This is called psychokinesis, or PK for short. The focus person is unaware that the force is coming from their own mind, in that it is a subconscious outlet. In the early 1970s it was thought the victim may be suffering frustration and tension, particularly of a sexual nature. But much firmer and more modern evidence would suggest a link not with sexual problems, but with a straightforward desire for attention. . ."

I snapped the book shut. That was the end of that theory. Neither Helen nor I had any desire to seek attention. Surely we were both well-balanced youngsters wanting for nothing. Okay, so I had gone through the agonies of puberty just like any other teenager—the periods of self-doubt, the feelings of isolation, anxiety over my exam options, the whole caboodle. But here I was, finished with A levels, moderately confident of doing well, happy with my home life. The idea that I was seeking attention was unthinkable.

And what about Helen? She was more than happy in her work, and she had a caring boyfriend in Mark Brody. Granted, she would like to see him a little more often, but the fact that he was at university 150 miles away meant their time together was limited.

Was I naïve in thinking that we did not have the problems that faced many other teenagers? Could either Helen or I be unhappy enough subconsciously to be sending out those distressing waves of power? I thought not.

*   *   *

"It was lovely," Helen enthused over dinner that night. "We cut across country through the Isle of Oxney and parked at Camber. We walked along the beach for ages towards the Wicks."

Dad smiled. "Too many people about for my liking at this time of year. I bet it was packed."

"It was rather busy," admitted Mark. "The only reason we walked so far along the beach was to try and find a place to spread our towels without disturbing anyone."

"Fibber," laughed Helen, pulling playfully at his meticulously combed blond locks. Mark gently gripped both her wrists.

"Now look here," he said with mock severity.

Helen giggled, looking happier than I had seen for the last couple of weeks. Mark taking her out for the day was the best therapy she could have had.

Her eyes shone as she peered into his face. "Yes, sir, I'm looking."

He let go of her left wrist and, speaking infinitely slowly, wagged his forefinger at her in rhythm with his words. "If you don't leave my hair alone you'll be in very serious trouble."

From the corner of my eye I spotted a swift movement outside the window. Even the split second it had taken to whirl my head in that direction was too long and it was gone by the time my eyes came to rest there. No one else seemed to notice it; they were all grinning at Mark and Helen playing out their charade.

Charade! What a charade we had been going through these last few days. But a charade was meant to be fun, wasn't it? "Fun" was definitely not a word that could be used to describe our experiences.

And here it was again, toying with us. That half-glimpsed fleeting movement was all we could see, and yet Mark had experienced an altogether more frightening confrontation with it. What did it want? What *could* it want from us? We were just an ordinary family, just like any other. We had lived happily at White Pastures for four years, undisturbed by any paranormal happenings until that night of my final A level exam.

Why was it coming now and why did it always bring an enigmatic, loathsome, oppressive feeling with it that vanished as swiftly as our visitor itself?

When I looked back at Helen a frown was creasing her brow and her eyes registered pain and surprise. "Mark!" she squealed, trying to prise his fingers off her wrist with her free hand. "Stop it. You're hurting me."

Suddenly Mark's arms shot up in the air and his chair tipped backwards, sending him crashing sickeningly to the floor. What happened next was shrouded in confusion and I'm sure was over too quickly for my mind to register it properly. What I thought happened was that as everyone leaped up, Mark's plate, laden with cold chicken and salad, raised itself into the air and smashed down onto his face.

By the time my senses recovered Helen and Sarah were both laughing at the sight of him lying on the floor covered with mayonnaise, lettuce, and tomato. But Dad looked angry. "What on earth are you playing at?" he snapped.

Wiping some of the thick creamy liquid away from his eyes Mark looked around bemused. "I don't know," he mumbled. "I thought someone grabbed my hand."

"That was me, silly." Helen was still giggling at him. "You started to squeeze a bit too much and you were hurting me, so I pushed your hand away."

Mark was examining the back of his fingers. "You scratched me hard enough, didn't you?"

The laughter died in Helen's throat. "I didn't scratch you. I pulled your fingers off my hand, that's all."

"Then who did this?" demanded Mark, stretching out his hand to reveal several deep gouges across the knuckles. Helen stared at the wounds, her eyes widening at the sight of blood oozing its way across the torn skin.

"I didn't do that," she gasped.

"I didn't squeeze you, either." Mark scrambled to his feet. "I felt you bending my fingers back and the next thing I knew you'd knocked me off my chair."

"I only tried to get your hand off when you started hurting me. I certainly didn't push you off the chair."

More mayonnaise trickled into Mark's eyes. He wiped it away and picked the plate off the carpet. "How did my dinner get down here?"

"Your arm caught it as you fell," I lied quickly, hoping the others hadn't seen it suddenly lift up of its own accord and home in accurately and fiercely on Mark's head.

Dad's severe expression began to crack as yet another dollop of mayonnaise trickled off the end of Mark's nose. "Let that be a lesson to you both. No more horseplay at the table. It's a wonder you didn't break anything."

Mark looked sheepish. "Yeah, I'm sorry Bob. It won't happen again."

Mum started to walk towards the door. "I'd better clean this mess up before it stains the carpet."

"No, let me do it," insisted Mark. "It's my fault. It's the least I can do."

I thought Mum gave in a little too easily. "Right," she said. "Thank you. You'll find a bucket and cloth under the sink."

With Mark safely out of earshot, Dad turned to Helen. "I meant what I said. No more horseplay. You could both have been hurt. You shouldn't have pushed him over like that."

"I didn't push him. I just. . .oh, I don't know what I did. I thought I only pulled his hand off my arm."

"Don't let it happen again."

Sarah was still giggling quietly. "He looked so funny with that salad all over him."

Dad started to say something, but his words were masked by a cry and a thud from just outside the dining room door. The sight waiting to greet us as we ran to the hall made us stop short with a jolt. Mark lay on his back, soaking wet, with a sodden cloth over his head and an upturned bucket alongside him.

"For goodness' sake, what's going on here tonight?" cried Dad, sounding more than a little irritated as he glared at the pool of water working its way into the carpet. Mark spluttered and hurled the rag away.

Helen, seeing he wasn't hurt, started laughing again, which only annoyed him all the more.

"It's not funny," he snapped. "Someone tipped that water all over me."

"You do seem to be accident-prone today," said Mum, and I guessed by the way her bottom lip was trembling that she was trying her hardest not to laugh.

"I'm telling you, someone tipped that water over me. They wrenched the bucket from my hands."

"Don't be silly." Helen's voice had lost its humour. "You must have slipped or tripped."

For the second time that night, Mark scrambled up. This time embarrassment and anger clouded his face. "I did not fall," he said slowly and firmly. "I was coming back from the kitchen when someone tugged at the bucket. It was pulled out of my hands and tipped over my head."

"Then what were you doing lying on the floor?" gasped Sarah between helpless peals of laughter.

"I was pushed," snapped Mark. "The bucket flew onto my head and someone knocked me backwards against the wall. He indicated a wet patch on the wall.

Dad shook his head angrily. "We were all in the dining room. No one could have pushed you." He strode off down the hall with the bucket.

"At least it's washed the dinner off you," said Sarah, still laughing.

Mark flicked his wet hair out of his eyes. "I'm going upstairs to get dry."

Helen giggled again, took hold of his arm, and they disappeared together in the direction of the bathroom.

CHAPTER 9: THE CAR

I AWOKE the next morning to the sound of an argument just outside my bedroom door. It was Dad's voice I heard first.

"They were on the hook where I always put them," he said. "I saw them when I locked up last night and put the door key alongside."

Then came Mum's contribution. "Are you sure you haven't left them in the car again?"

"What do you mean, 'again'?" Dad sounded quite hurt by her barbed attack. "I've only ever locked my keys in the car once. And that was because I thought you'd taken them out."

"That's right. Blame me."

"I'm not blaming you. All I'm saying is—"

"I know very well what you're saying. You're saying it's my fault you've lost your keys."

"I've not lost them. I put them on the hook last night."

"Then where are they?"

"If you've not moved them, then the kids must have."

The next moment he flung my bedroom door open, stormed over, and began shaking my shoulders.

"Have you seen my keys?" he demanded.

"Uh?" I feigned sleep, but he only shook me harder.

"Have you moved my car keys?"

"Wassup?" I groaned, hauling myself up onto my elbows and peering sleepily at him.

"My keys," he repeated. "Have you seen them?"

"No. Why? Have you lost them?"

"I have not lost them," he snapped as a red flush washed over his face. "I put them on the hook last night and now they've gone."

"I've not moved them. Why would I want to move them?"

"I don't know. But someone has."

"Don't go on at me, I've not touched them."

"Can you help me look for them, please?" His tone was friendlier now. "I'll be late for work."

Mum popped her head round the door. "Where's the spare set?"

"At the office. I thought I'd be more likely to lose them there than at home."

Mum cast her eyes heavenward and disappeared down the passage.

"Have you looked in the dining room?" I asked as I climbed out of bed.

"I've spent the last ten minutes looking everywhere. They've simply vanished."

"Are you sure you brought them in last night?"

"Quite sure. I remember putting them on the hook as soon as I came in. And they were still there when I locked the kitchen door last night."

I left him heading for his bedroom to check through the pockets of the suit he wore yesterday, while I went downstairs. A faint rumbling noise met my ears as soon as I opened the kitchen door. It was a familiar sound, one I'd heard many times. It seemed to be coming from outside.

"Dad!" I shouted, running to the foot of the stairs. "Dad, come quickly."

There was a commotion upstairs as everyone scrambled along the landing, Sarah from her en suite where she was getting ready for school, and Mark and Helen from his and her respective bedrooms, rubbing sleep from their eyes.

"What is it?" called Dad as he started to come down.

"In the kitchen," I cried. "Quickly though." I ran through. Yes, I could still hear it.

"What is it?" he asked again as he joined me.

"Listen."

We stood absolutely still, straining to hear the faint rumbling, which was now much quieter than when I first heard it.

"It's coming from the garage," said Mark.

"It's the car engine," Dad shouted. "What the hell's going on?"

He almost flew outside and fumbled frantically to unlock the garage side door. By the time he had the door open we were just behind him, but the noise had stopped. He squeezed between the wall and the gleaming red Rover until he got to the driver's door. Then he let out a yell and reached inside.

"Look." He held up his car keys, mystified. "They were in here after all. I don't understand that."

"But who started the engine?" asked Mark.

"It must have been another car we heard," said Mum with a logic that only mothers seemed capable of. "It was probably going past in the lane."

"I could have sworn it came from in here." Dad scratched his head. "You must be right, though. And yet I was so sure I brought these in with me last night."

Something caught my eye. "I think it was your car we just heard."

"No, it couldn't have been," Dad insisted. "Your mother's right. It must have been a car in the lane."

Shaking my head, I pointed to a few drops of water on the floor, just behind the twin exhaust pipes. Dad turned pale as he looked in the direction of my finger.

"What does that mean?" Mum wanted to know.

"It's condensation, Jean," explained Mark. "When a cold engine starts it blows a few drops of water out of the exhaust. This engine's been on in the last couple of minutes."

"Perhaps the water's still there from yesterday." Helen sounded as if she were hunting wildly for any suitable explanation.

"No, it's fresh," said Dad. Even as we watched, the tiny droplets began drying out.

Mum gripped his arm. "Bob, there must be someone in the garage."

Dad walked round the back of the Rover to Mum's Nissan parked next to it and peered carefully inside. Then he bobbed down to look under both cars.

"There's no one here," he announced as he straightened up. Then he faced Mum. "I must go or I'll be late. Please be careful today. I know it's going to be hot again, but keep the doors locked and the windows shut. I'll ring the police and tell them what's happened as soon as I get to the office. They might want to come and look around the garage."

They didn't. Dad phoned us an hour later to say he explained to the police how the keys had been taken from the hook and found in the car, and how the engine was switched on, then suddenly off again, but they sounded somewhat cynical, wanting to know if he were absolutely certain he'd taken the keys in with him last night.

"But what about the water on the floor, Dad? Did you tell them about that? Surely that proves the engine had been on."

Dad's voice crackled back down the line. "They said it could have come from anywhere, Simon. And looking at it from their point of view, what are they supposed to think? I assured them no one was in the garage and both doors were locked when we got there. We can't really expect them to drop everything just because we thought we heard the engine running."

"I suppose not." Deep in my heart I really had wanted them to find a rational explanation.

* * *

Mark and Helen went out for the day again in Mum's car. They asked me to go with them, but I was in no mood for playing gooseberry. And anyway, they probably only asked me out of politeness.

Instead, I planned to do some more sunbathing. Examining myself in the full-length mirror, I noted with some satisfaction that my tan was coming on nicely. I mentally counted the weeks until my holiday in the middle of August. Just over eight. Then I would be off to Paleokastritsa in Corfu with a couple of schoolfriends. Fortunately, Dad was heavily subsidising my contribution to the financial arrangements, saying it was his treat for all the hard work I had put in for my A levels. By the time we would be ready to go, I expected I would be sporting the best suntan I'd ever had. But it seemed Mum had other ideas, at least for the moment.

"Seeing as how I'm housebound again today," she called from downstairs, "I may as well blanche some fruit and vegetables for the freezer. Could you pop down to the village for me, please?"

"Yes, give me a couple of minutes."

* * *

I returned home about forty-five minutes later heavily laden with baskets. Mum was standing by the table that contained her scales, several baking trays, chopping board, and a selection of knives. She looked puzzled.

"That's funny. I know I put my big saucepan on the cooker." She walked over to the cupboards on the far side of the room and opened each of them in turn. Two saucepan racks were inside, and I could see all the spaces were filled except one.

"Look here," she mumbled, pointing to the gap. "I took that saucepan out two minutes ago. Where's it gone? Can you see it?" She scanned the kitchen.

"You're as bad as Dad with the keys," I laughed. But my jovial appearance concealed a worried doubt. My parents were too well organised to lose things like keys and saucepans. What's more, the sound that morning had definitely been Dad's car. I knew I hadn't been mistaken about the Rover's distinctive purr.

"I put it on the cooker," Mum said, bringing my thoughts up to date in a flash. "Saucepans don't just vanish like that."

But this one had. If it was still in the kitchen it had found a fucking good hiding place. Eventually we gave up the search and Mum was forced to use a different pan instead.

I spent the afternoon on a lounger soaking up the powerful rays, my mind going over everything that had happened. What had begun as something mysterious but harmless, even something of a joke, had fast become a frightening and potentially dangerous nightmare. I was pleased Mark would be staying with us for another week and a half to keep Helen occupied, and Sarah's thoughts seemed to be filled more than adequately with young Steve.

The atmosphere at dinner that evening wasn't so much strained as simply tense, probably because we were all silently recalling our experiences of the day before. Mark endeavoured to be cheerful as he reflected on how he and Helen spent another wonderful day at the coast, this time at Dymchurch in St Mary's Bay, between Dungeness and Folkestone.

"We're going to Brighton tomorrow," Helen enthused. "Do come with us, Simon."

"You don't want me along," I protested. "I'm quite happy sunbathing here."

"Do come," Mark insisted. "We really would like you to."

Mum looked up from her portion of pineapple pavlova. "You go with them. And if they end up anywhere near that nudist beach drag them in the opposite direction."

CHAPTER 10: DEADLY PRESENCE

WE WERE UP at the crack of dawn so that Helen could fix a picnic while I pored over the map. Not that I didn't know my way to Brighton—we'd been many times and I knew all the main routes—but I planned to take the side roads to avoid the holiday crowds.

I wanted to drive, but having passed my test only six weeks earlier, Mum insisted on either Mark or Helen taking the wheel. Helen said that as she had prepared the food she wanted to relax in the back, so I settled in to the passenger seat with the atlas on my knee and Mark pulled us off the drive just after nine o'clock.

The first part of the journey was easy-going as Mark drove steadily through the countryside towards Heathfield. Once we passed through the town we began to encounter more traffic, and the B2192 into Lewes was as busy as I had ever seen it. It took us marginally over half an hour to reach the A27 Brighton road on the other side.

Just before we got to the seafront, I spotted a road to our left that would bypass the cars queuing to get through the centre. "Down here," I said, pointing to the narrow street. Mark swung the Nissan round the corner and we headed away from the town towards Rottingdean. "Now along here." I instructed Mark to hang a right. "And next right as well. Then park anywhere you can by the model railway."

We hardly had to go more than a couple of hundred yards before we saw a car pulling away from a space, and Mark manoeuvred effortlessly into the vacant spot.

"Hey, we're here," he cried, switching off the engine. "It's been ages since I've been to Brighton."

Helen, in her yellow vest top and matching shorts, was out of the car first and hammering on the hatchback tailgate.

"Come on, open up," she squealed to Mark. "Pull the little lever on the floor."

Mark obeyed and watched in the rearview mirror as the hatch swung up. Helen started ferreting around and by the time Mark and I were alongside her, she had fetched out two of the three sun loungers, the picnic basket, and the bag containing towels and swimming costumes.

The sun was hot and high in the sky. I could feel it burning my arms and legs. We hurried on to the shingle and quickly found a spot to make camp for the day. Then we tried to conceal what nature gave us (not altogether successfully) behind towels while we wriggled out of our shorts and into bathing costumes.

"I don't know why we're bothering with towels," grunted Mark, trying to keep his from falling, while hoisting his trunks. "We're not far from the nudist beach."

Helen giggled while struggling with her own blue and white towel, which seemed determined to develop a will of its own. I smiled, looking around at the throng of happy holidaymakers enjoying the sun. They stretched away in both directions along the pebbly beach, ranging from the painfully thin through the slightly tubby, to the downright obese. Their various shades of skin tone showed as almost pure white in those who had obviously just arrived, to the smooth golden brown of those who'd had more time to absorb the powerful ultraviolet rays with which we had been blessed for three weeks.

Away to our left the cloudless sky was a delicate pale, almost hazy, blue that gradually developed into a deep royal hue the further it stretched towards Hove. The wind had hardly enough breath to ripple a millpond let alone the jewelled and sparkling surface of the English Channel, whose waters lapped gently at the millions upon millions of stones that composed this stretch of coastline. A few hundred yards to the right of where we lay, the famous Brighton Pier, a once majestic memento of the British seaside heritage, stretched its slender, but increasingly shabby, arm into the reflected blue.

I finished smothering myself with lemon-smelling sun oil and passed the bottle to Helen who started to rub the sticky fluid gently across Mark's back. Her face showed nothing but carefree happiness.

Until we fathomed what was going on, the more we kept Helen away from home, the better off she'd be. We had to make sure her time was filled in order to keep her mind off our dark intruder. I smiled at the thought of the look that would surely creep over her face during her birthday party next Saturday when Dad produced the replacement presents he was going to pick up. On the night the original ones disappeared, she had said, between sobs, not to bother getting her anything else, but simply to make sure the party was a success. Glumly, we had nodded our acceptance, but I guessed that we were all making up our minds that no way were we going to let Helen have a birthday without presents.

I eased back in the lounger and clicked the headrest into place. I glanced sideways to make sure the towels were covering the picnic basket, a somewhat feeble effort to keep the food as cool as possible.

Slowly I started drifting towards a fitful doze, helped by the sun that was creating an almost hypnotic warm glow throughout my body, and the rhythmic sounds of children playing a game of French cricket with a softball and a tennis racquet.

What seemed like just a few moments, but my watch told me was an hour and a half, had passed when Helen roused me by none-too-gently ruffling my hair.

"Wake up, dozy chops. Time for lunch."

Mark was busy pouring three plastic tumblers of orange juice from the thermos flask, which was just as adept at keeping drinks cool as keeping them hot, and the food was already laid out on a blanket. There were individual pork pies, three flavours of crisps, a mound of scotch eggs with pickle, some of my favourite garlic pate sandwiches, slices of cold roast pork and beef, and an orange and apple for each of us.

I noticed that Mark poured a liberal amount of vodka into each tumbler of juice.

It has always been my confirmed and often proven belief that food tastes better when eaten outside, and I swear that there wasn't a more superior meal consumed anywhere in the land that day. By the time we finished and packed everything away, it was almost three o'clock and the sun was getting on for two-thirds of the way down the sky, but still showed no signs of losing power.

Another luxurious doze took the clock round to half past four. This time it was Mark who roused me. "Come on, Simon. We're going for a dip before setting off."

I daresay the water temperature was quite high as the sun had been glaring down on it mercilessly for twenty-two days, but when a renegade wave swept over my trunks it still came as a quite a shock.

"It's gorgeous," gasped Helen, thrusting forward into the rippling blue. I decided that as the ice was already broken, so to speak, there was little point dawdling any further. I took a deep breath and threw myself into the depths. The water stung my skin like a thousand tiny needles for a few seconds before turning into a soothing relaxant. A few determined and fast-moving strokes of the front crawl became a gentler breaststroke, and then I turned lazily in the water and floated on my back.

Helen and Mark were already about twenty-five yards further out, happily splashing each other. I turned over again and started to tread water; I could barely touch the bottom.

Suddenly, as I looked on, Mark's head shot under the surface. Even from a distance I could hear Helen giggling as she slapped the palms of both hands sharply against the surface of the water, like I had taught her, to make loud pops in the ears of underwater swimmers. It must have been twenty seconds before Mark came up for air, coughing and sputtering, and appeared to be trying to shout. His words were lost amidst a gurgling as he went under again. Helen was still laughing, but her arms were windmilling through the water as she backstroked away from the area of Mark's playful fooling.

I kept my eyes on the spot where he went under for the second time and saw him rocket upwards like a cork from a bottle. Whoa! He came clean out of the water, body arcing over, and then tumbling back heavily with an almighty splash. I watched in total disbelief as he sank for a third time.

There's absolutely no way he could do that, I told myself. *He's too far from the shore to launch himself that high.* My stomach knotted, telling me something was wrong.

"Helen," I cried at the top of my voice. "Where's Mark?"

She didn't seem to hear me and continued to swim away from him, parallel to the beach.

"Helen! Go back to Mark!" As my cry died away a pair of arms reached up from the sea, flailing frantically. Then Mark's head broke through the surface. The air was rent by his screams for help. Then he was under once more in a cloud of spray, his helpless cries lost amidst a flurry of gurgling.

I sucked in as much air as my lungs would take and dived into the underwater world. My eyes swiftly grew accustomed to the strange perspective and I was able to see Mark struggling vainly to reach the surface. He was in an upright position, kicking wildly with his left leg. The other leg was stiff, pointing straight down, and before I could reach him he bent low and was bashing at his right ankle with both fists as if trying to free it from the grip of some unseen vice. A mass of bubbles escaped from his mouth, making their way to the surface. As I drew nearer, I could see his eyes bulging in their sockets, his blond hair streaming upwards as if vainly directing him in the direction he needed to take.

He continued beating at his right ankle and started rubbing his left foot up and down his calf. *What was he trying to kick away?*

I arrived within a few inches of his writhing body, and, taking hold of his arm, tried to steer him upwards. It appeared he was doing his best to go with me but it was like pulling a ten-ton weight. I yanked for all I was worth until I was afraid I would tear his arm from its shoulder, but he remained rooted to the spot. As I released him, he grabbed my wrist and pointed to his leg. I nodded, indicating I understood he wanted me to haul him up by his legs, and I dropped down to the seabed.

His right leg was utterly and completely immobile. No amount of pulling or pushing could move it, but nothing was holding it there. Nothing that I could see, anyway. Putting both hands round his ankle, I tried to channel all my power into the relevant muscles. For a couple of seconds nothing happened. I might as well have been trying to push a mighty oak over. Then all resistance suddenly vanished. We both shot forward at least two yards. Before I could drag myself to a halt, I felt both my wrists being grabbed and torn away from Mark's foot.

I spun backwards and the watery void danced around me in a circle.

My head and heart were pounding, my lungs burning like fire, screaming for a fresh supply of oxygen. I saw that Mark had now pushed through the surface. He'd been down much longer than me, but I didn't think I could survive another second without taking an immediate breath.

I broke through into the air, gulping in a mouthful of salty water in the haste to replenish my lungs. Coughing it out, I managed to splutter a few words. "Are you okay?"

A torrent of water spurted from his mouth, rendering him unable to speak. By now Helen had arrived.

"What happened?" she cried, reaching for Mark's arm.

All I wanted to do at that moment was draw in huge lungfuls of beautiful, sweet, life-giving air. "Get him to the beach," I managed to gasp between coughs.

Helen's swimming expertise gave her the confidence to take immediate command of the situation. "Float on your back, Mark." He weakly complied, and she cupped a hand under his chin and began a powerful sidestroke towards the shore, pulling him effortlessly behind her.

My tortured lungs rattled and grated but began to feel a little more normal as the air started to expel any water left in them. On turning towards the shingle, I could see the water's edge was crowded with people who'd witnessed part of the drama and were on their way to help us. By the time I could feel land beneath my feet and managed to wade ashore, a tall, powerfully-built man had whisked Mark back to our towels and was slapping him hard on the back. I hurried over as fast as the unforgiving shingle would allow and found Mark spluttering his thanks to the concerned crowd standing over him.

"No lasting damage," said the back slapper. "The water's out of your system now."

"Yeah," gasped Mark, still somewhat winded and breathless and finding it difficult to draw the long, easy breaths he craved. "I'll be okay soon."

"What happened?" asked the man, bobbing down in front of him. "Did you get a cramp out there?"

Before Mark could answer, the mother of two young children who had been sitting next to us piped up rather brusquely. "More than likely. They had a good meal not long before going in. You should never go into the sea on a full stomach. Guaranteed to bring on the cramp, doing that."

Mark seemed grateful for her suggestion and clung to it. "I reckon that's what it was," he agreed, speaking more evenly now. "I did eat a fair bit."

The people who'd gathered round us could see he was recovering and began to trail away, muttering to each other. No doubt this little bit of excitement would give them something to talk about for a while.

I started to gather up the towels and push them into the bag. "Come on, we'd better be getting home."

Gingerly, Helen eased Mark to his feet, but he winced as soon as he started to walk, his face creasing into a mask of pain. "My ankle," he gasped. Two vivid bruises the size of fifty pence coins marked the inside of his right ankle a couple of inches apart.

Seeing the rings of darkened skin made me suddenly aware of a dull ache in my wrists. I glanced down and saw to my horror that the base of both my forearms bore similar wounds. Helen's eyes followed my stunned gaze and widened in surprise.

"Your hands. They're bruised, as well."

Mark's warning glance to me, as if to say play along with the cramp story, was completely unnecessary.

"I, er, guess Mark must have kicked me while I was trying to get him to the surface." I sounded unconvincing, but if Helen noticed my hesitation she didn't say anything. My senses reeled with the thought of what really happened and what it meant.

It was as if whatever had kept Mark imprisoned beneath the surface had angrily taken hold of my wrists with steel pincers and thrown me away from him. We made our way back up the shingle to the car, Mark leaning heavily on Helen's shoulder.

My thoughts turned back to the minute or so I spent underwater, especially to how Mark's leg appeared to be fastened firmly in some invisible clamp. I examined the red and blue marks on my wrists, which looked like indentations caused by a thumb and finger squeezing hard on that particularly bony part of my arm.

The implications coursed through me like wildfire. This was no accident. Mark hadn't suffered a cramp. Some unseen entity had held him down there and fought my attempts to free him. It must be connected with what we had come to accept as a supernatural force at our home, but this threw a totally different and more sinister light on the picture. It seemed our spirit or poltergeist, whatever it was, was focused on Mark, Helen, and me and wasn't restricted to our home or grounds, but could wander at will, plaguing us wherever we were.

And it had shown its true colours at last. No longer was it content to put in fleeting, harmless appearances interspersed with what could possibly be taken for childish pranks; it had revealed a malevolent and dangerous aspect. No longer could we shrug its presence off as being merely irritating. It had tried to kill Mark and we had to view it as hostile, liable to strike at us both inside our home and out.

We were not safe anywhere.

* * *

When we arrived at the car, Mark reached into a zipped pocket in his trunks for the keys and handed them to Helen. "I'm not going to be able to drive," he said. "I need to rest my ankle."

I held out my hand. "I'll drive. I'll be alright."

Helen looked doubtful. "I don't know. Mum did say you weren't to."

"And I wouldn't if this hadn't happened. You sit in the back with Mark. If you like we can swap a couple of miles from home so you're driving when we arrive."

She still looked uncertain. Then she passed the keys over to me. "Okay. But be careful."

"Of course I will."

We fished our shorts and T-shirts out of the bag and hauled them over our damp swimming costumes before getting in the car. I revved the engine. This would be the furthest I'd driven. Under normal circumstances I'd have relished the prospect of driving so far but I felt distinctly uneasy after all that had happened.

Dismissing the fears as groundless overspill from my earlier worries, I reversed the Nissan out of the parking space and we set off for home. Mark sat immediately behind me and I could see in the rearview mirror that Helen lay her head on his shoulder.

It was too early to catch the day-trippers going home, but a few office workers swelled the traffic on the A27 out of Brighton and it took us a few moments to clear the town.

"Was it really cramp?" Helen asked as we picked up the A26 on the homeward side of Lewes. I caught Mark's glance in the mirror and saw him nod.

"It must have been," he said. "I felt a sharp pain in my stomach, which virtually crippled me. If Simon hadn't got to me when he did. . .I don't like to think what might have happened."

I kept strictly within the speed limit, even on the open B road between Ringmer and Cross In Hand when I was tempted to see exactly what the Nissan could do.

I craned my neck a couple of times to catch a glimpse in the mirror of Mark and Helen who'd fallen asleep. Their gentle rhythmic breathing grew slightly deeper as we crossed the county boundary back into Kent.

It was a good feeling, purring along, sometimes being overtaken by speeding cars, even occasionally overtaking slow ones myself. I'd only driven short distances previously, and as we swallowed up the miles I needed all my concentration to combat the drowsiness creeping into me. I'd had the driver's window half-open for the last few miles but now wound it down fully, enjoying the refreshing blast of air. I could still feel my eyes closing, though, and it was a real effort to stop them from shutting.

Even shaking my head violently only brought me back to full alertness for a few seconds before the weariness was back.

As if something were telling me that it was okay to go to sleep.

Gentle.

Soothing.

Join Mark and Helen. Asleep, it seemed to be saying.

Sleep. Sleep. Sleep.

It was like being pleasantly merry. Surely it couldn't have been the effects of the vodka I'd drunk on the beach. Half of me kept fighting the feeling.

Wake up, for fuck's sake, insisted one inner voice.

But the other half of me. . . .

No, said another, much more soothing inner voice. *Go to sleep.*

You know you want to.

You're drowsy.

You want to doze.

It's okay. Doze.

If only for a few seconds.

You'll wake refreshed.

Shaking my head, I raised my eyebrows as high as they would go in an effort to stop my eyes slipping shut. I tried to read the speedometer but the dial swam crazily around the dashboard. The road was now hurtling beneath the windscreen at a frantic pace.

But all I wanted to do was sleep.

Vaguely, I saw the dot swing round the bend about 300 yards in front of us, growing rapidly all the time until it took the shape of a car. Hurtling ever nearer. Nearer. Nearer.

A single powerful and penetrating note launched a vicious assault on my ears, drowning out the insistent words that were still trying to lull me to sleep. Suddenly I saw two beams of bright light flashing angrily and constantly.

Headlights. A car horn.

The car heading straight for us was no more than a few yards away, braking, swerving sharply.

In the split second when my senses returned and I hauled the wheel round, I caught sight of a man's malicious face leering at me in the mirror. It was a face of utmost evil, but was gone before I had time to register its features. All that showed in the mirror now were Helen and Mark being jerked around by the car's sudden erratic spinning.

My feet jabbed at the brake and clutch, and with a protesting squeal of burning rubber I somehow managed to guide the Nissan past the oncoming vehicle with half an inch to spare. We came to a halt with a body-lurching jerk, flinging my passengers into a heap against the nearside.

I whirled round, but there was no sign of anyone in the back except Mark and Helen.

"What the hell's going on?" demanded Mark.

In order to spare Helen, I felt honesty would not be the best policy at that moment. I would tell Mark the truth later, but for now a lie would have to suffice.

"Something ran into the road. A fox, I think. I swerved to miss it."

Helen rubbed her left elbow, which had taken a crack against the side of the car. "Thank goodness you didn't cause any damage," she said. "You'd better let me drive now."

"No, it's okay. I'm. . ." I was going to say I was alright and could carry on, but the recollection of that awful face sprang into my mind's eye. "Maybe it would be better." Again I hesitated. What if the face appeared in the mirror while Helen was driving?

Then again, perhaps I was overtired and imagined that leering grin.

"Yes, actually I am a little drowsy, if you don't mind?"

"I think you'd better straighten up first," suggested Mark.

For the first time since we screeched to a halt, I took my bearings. We'd come to rest at an angle of about forty-five degrees, with the rear nearside wheel half a yard across the grass verge. I manoeuvred to a parking position and got out.

Skid marks from the opposite side of the road showed how we'd swerved across the white line to our own part of the highway. I froze with horror at the thought of the near miss. I don't know how long we'd been on the wrong side, but I did know it must have been our unwelcome visitor making another attempt on our lives.

Helen had already clambered over the seat into the front and was adjusting the mirror.

"Look," I began hesitantly. "Perhaps I'd better drive, after all. You've just been sleeping and I'm wide awake."

Again I heard the inner voice. Its tone mocking. *Sleep, sleep, sleep.* Then it was gone. But a chilling laugh lasted another second or two in my head.

"No," Helen said. "I'll drive now."

"It wasn't my fault. If I'd hit that fox I might've lost control and we'd have had an accident. I did manage to stop safely, didn't I?" I pointed to the bonnet. "The engine's still running. It was a perfect emergency stop."

Her eyes narrowed a little as she looked up at me through the open window. "Get in the back."

If the face did come again and she panicked, I'd be in a better position to gain control of the car if I were in the front. Without a word, I walked round and slid in alongside her. She selected first gear and released the handbrake, and as she eased her foot off the clutch we slid smoothly away.

I turned to look at Mark in the back. "Not a word to Mum and Dad about our escapade in the water."

"Nor your fox," said Helen.

"I agree. We don't want to worry them."

CHAPTER 11: DEMONIC ACTION

I HEARD DAD LEAVE for work the next morning just a few moments before Mark's tuneless whistling floated down the landing. It wasn't long before he knocked softly on my door.

It was the first time we'd been able to get together alone. Dad had taken us out for a drink the previous night, and we'd gone straight to bed when we got back. In one respect I was glad; the trip to the pub had kept Helen away from home and her thoughts away from our troubles. But it also meant Mark and I hadn't been able to discuss what happened at the beach or for me to tell him the truth about our near miss.

"I was swimming normally," he recalled, "when I was pulled under. At first I thought it was you or Helen fooling around, but then I could see there was no one down there with me."

I shuddered at the memory of my wrists being grabbed by those same unseen hands.

His eyes looked beyond me, beyond my window. "I tried desperately to get back to the surface but something was definitely holding me down. Suddenly my legs were free and it was almost as if I were being thrown out of the water. I remember sinking again and being held under. I don't think I came up again, did I, until you got me away from it?"

He sounded so calm, just as if we were discussing the fortunes of our favourite soccer teams instead of something unknown that had tried to kill him.

Then I told him how I became unnaturally drowsy while driving home and about the face in the mirror.

That piqued his interest. "Are you sure? Could your mind have been playing tricks as you were so tired?"

What could I say? I only saw it for a second, if that, just as my senses returned on the brink of the crash.

"I suppose it's just like all the other inexplicable things that have happened."

My thoughts returned to something the Reverend McBeil had told me on Monday. "I wonder if we should take the vicar up on his suggestion that he have a look here. We all accept that there is a ghost, or something supernatural, so it can't do any harm for him to come and see."

"I suppose not. Why don't you give him a call and see when he can come. Then I'll make sure Helen's out."

But I was no longer sure that we were doing the right thing by keeping Helen cocooned. "It might not be a bad idea if she stays while he's here," I said. "The fact that this thing can leave the house and follow us seems to indicate that somehow it's involved with you, me, or Helen."

Mark didn't seem convinced, though. "If the vicar were a proven psychic or ghost hunter or something I might agree with you. But he's not. He's coming as an ordinary man."

"He's coming as a clergyman," I countered, "to see if there's anything evil here, something that doesn't belong. If it is connected to one of us, it'll make his task easier if we're all here."

Mark shook his head. "It would be simpler if we followed Sherlock Holmes's old adage of a process of elimination. Let me take Helen away when the vicar comes and if he doesn't find anything we'll suggest she and I meet him. That way, if it's only connected with you, Helen won't be put through an ordeal for nothing."

"I'm sure she'd want to be here."

"You've told me yourself how ill she looked before I came when all this started, and she seems much better while we've helped her avoid thinking about it."

I had to agree with him on that score.

"And what's more," he continued, "I think you'll have difficulty persuading her to see him if she knows why he's coming. I tried to get her to talk about it when you first told me what'd been happening and she wouldn't."

I remembered the conversation I overheard in the kitchen a few days ago, Helen's tearful response when he had urged her to talk it over with him.

"Simon, if I honestly thought it would do any good I'd say yes, bring the vicar in to see us all, including Helen. But the way she's clamming up means that deep down she's very frightened. I just think it'd do more harm than good right now."

"It would be a way of getting to the bottom of it, or at least making some headway, if the vicar does come up with something."

"I agree, and I'll make sure she sees him if he doesn't find anything without us. But if he does find something, Helen won't be distressed unnecessarily."

His argument certainly made sense. Yesterday's events told me there was a lot more danger connected with our spiritual visitor than we previously thought. I remembered lying in bed a few nights ago thinking that a ghost could be good fun.

How wrong I was.

* * *

Mum said she must put in an appearance at the hospital shop and left in her car shortly after nine thirty in the morning. Helen wanted to sunbathe but Mark talked her into going for a walk by the river so I'd be free to call the vicar.

The number in Mum's address book was only a couple of digits different from ours. Slowly I dialled it, listening for the ringing tone. It could only have shrilled its summons at the vicarage once before being answered.

"Meriton Vicarage, good morning."

"Good morning, Mrs. Jackson. This is Simon Reynolds. I came to see the Reverend McBeil the other day. Is he in, please?"

"He is," she crackled back. "Just one moment while I collect him."

Collect him! She made him sound like the mail.

There was a pause of about forty-five seconds. Then, "Hello Simon." The tone of just those two words reflected a certain amount of worry.

"I'm sorry to bother you," I said, "but you did say I could ask you to look around White Pastures if things got worse."

"What's happened?" His voice was quick, tense, and alert.

"Quite a lot since I saw you. Could you come over, please?"

"Of course. I'll just check my diary." He made it sound as if next week would do. I wanted him at White Pastures immediately.

"It is urgent," I snapped, instantly regretting the harshness of my tone. "I was rather hoping you'd come today," I added lamely.

"I will come today, but I've already got an appointment this morning and I was just going to see what time that is."

"Sorry," I muttered. "I thought. . ."

"It's alright, Simon. Don't worry." There was a pause, presumably while he swept his eyes across the page of his diary. "Yes, here we are. Eleven o'clock. I shouldn't be more than half an hour there, so shall we say quarter to twelve?"

"That's fine." I'm sure my voice clearly indicated relief.

"What is it?" he asked. "What's happened?"

"There's definitely something here," I told him. "It's started attacking us."

For a long time there was no answer and I feared we'd been cut off. "Mr. McBeil, are you still there?"

"Simon, listen very carefully. If you sense it in the house again before I arrive, get out straight away. Don't hesitate. Just get out. Do you understand? I'll be with you at quarter to twelve."

The sooner the better as far as I was concerned. I took Titus into the garden to play with him listlessly for half an hour. It seemed I was looking at my watch every ten minutes, each time feeling that an hour must have passed. Then I tried to relax on a sun lounger, but the vicar's warning had worried me considerably. He obviously felt we were in danger. Until that moment, I'd been hoping I was wrong and that spirits didn't behave maliciously. But the Reverend McBeil's concern had been paramount, and if anyone knew about the power of things beyond the grave it would surely be a man of the church.

After a fashion, the sight of Titus sleeping alongside me served as reassurance. He'd always been acutely uncomfortable when *it* was around. In the wake of Reverend McBeil's warning, I knew it would be prudent to keep Titus with us at all times until we solved the mystery. I made a mental note to put the idea to Dad, who up until then had never let the dog go into the lounge. Patting his head, I looked at the time again. Still only quarter to eleven.

It seemed impossible that an hour could take so long to pass; it was dragging forever. But eventually my watch said 11:50 a.m. He was late!

At 12:05 the impatient side of my nature came through—I couldn't stand it any longer and rang the vicarage again.

"Hello, Mrs. Jackson, it's Simon Reynolds again. Is the vicar there, please?"

"No, he left over an hour ago. He is coming to see you, but I know he was going to Ragstone Farm first to finalise plans for the summer fête next week."

"Perhaps he's got held up there. Okay, thanks, Mrs. Jackson."

Out in the garden again, time continued to crawl. Eventually, from the house, came the sound of a ringing bell. I ran inside to the front door.

"Mr. McBeil," I said, standing aside for him to come in. "I was—"

He held up his hand. "Sorry I'm late. I got delayed at Mr. Jebson's and cycled over as fast as I could." Sweat poured off his brow. His words, like his breath, came in rough, uneven bursts.

"Would you like a beer?" I asked. "Or some lemonade to cool off?"

"Lemonade, please." He started to cough, which turned his already florid face an even deeper shade. "I'm so sorry. I just couldn't get away."

Eventually he managed to quell the irritation in his lungs brought on by the exertion of cycling the two miles from Ragstone Farm to White Pastures as fast as he could in the blistering heat. His haste to reach us was another indication that he was taking these new developments very seriously.

"Let's go and sit in the kitchen," I suggested, "and I'll get your lemonade."

He followed me through the hall and sat at the table, breathing heavily, while I poured half a pint of lemonade. He drained it without a pause, readily accepting my invitation for a second. After a couple of draughts from the top-up, his eyes narrowed behind the dark-rimmed spectacles. "Now, Simon, what's happening?"

I told him in detail about the ransacking of our bedrooms, Mark's dinner plate and water tipping over him, the escapade with Dad's car keys, and our experiences in the sea at Brighton and on the way home.

"The house is empty," he stated. "I don't sense anything here at all."

It's not here now, I wanted to scream. *It comes and goes.* But I actually said, rather lamely, "Don't forget it followed us to Brighton. It's not restricted to the house."

"We need to deal in reality. I have had some experience with hauntings and possession; I do know what I'm talking about. Satan loves to deal in lies and the make-believe. The result can be devastation and chaos." His words chilled me to the bone, even though I didn't fully understand them.

"However, demonic activity doesn't have to focus on one physical spot," he continued. "It can be aimed at a specific person, but such events are usually triggered when the person in question is about to oppose Satan's power. Have any of you suffered headaches recently, had irrational fears, or a sense of unreality and disorientation?"

Irrational fears, certainly, I thought to myself, *especially when we first started seeing this thing. Unreality and disorientation? That described what happened to me in the car yesterday. Headaches? Not that anyone had mentioned.*

"Some of those things, yes," I said.

He looked grave, but puzzled, too. "What about a feeling of cold, and a stabbing or gripping sensation around the heart?"

Dumbly I shook my head.

"The early events you described—the movement outside the window, the face looking in, the dark shape—all seem to indicate that your house is the focus of a demonic attack. But yesterday's experiences would lead me to believe that the attack is against just one person. It's confusing; there are no clear signs either way."

"You make it sound as if this sort of thing happens regularly?"

"More regularly than you might think, especially against the church and the clergy."

"But why?"

"Against people such as yourselves, I don't know. Against the church, because we fight Satan and his ways. I've been involved in a few cases." He looked around the kitchen for several moments, seeming to probe every corner.

He'd told me a few moments earlier that there was nothing in our house. I wanted to know how he was so sure. In reply, he told me about an exorcism he had carried out recently. "There was an overpowering sense of evil, unease, and foreboding in that house. One room was much colder than the others. At the end of the ceremony the whole house seemed several degrees warmer and there was just a sensation of emptiness; the evil had gone."

"And you feel our house is empty? Like the other one felt after the exorcism?"

"I didn't really mean 'empty' in the traditional way. Before the exorcism there was a definite aura about the place, but afterwards it disappeared, leaving warmth, even a touch of humanity, in its wake." He paused to take another drink. "The best way to describe it is that when I arrived it was like walking into a room full of silent people you could sense but couldn't see. There was an overwhelming sensation that all was not as it should be, that the building wasn't quite right. The unease in those circumstances is so strong that no one who has ever experienced it will ever laugh at anyone else claiming to have felt it. The intensity of the feeling varies according to the power of the spirit and what its purpose is in being there. If it's wholly evil, there's often a nauseous smell accompanied by what's known as a cold spot."

I looked across at him, marvelling at his wealth of knowledge, wondering at the incredible tales he could probably tell. And all this from the vicar of a small rural parish.

"A what?"

"A cold spot. It can be either one particular spot or an entire room that's subjected to an intense stabbing of cold whenever the evil is present. And the longer the spirit is allowed to fester in one place, the more powerful it becomes and the more difficult it is to dislodge. Until the entity makes its presence felt physically, the description of 'silent people' fits perfectly. In the case I'm referring to, by the time I'd finished the exorcism it was as if those silent people had all left."

"And you don't feel we've got any of those silent people in our house?"

"Not at the moment. But that doesn't mean they haven't been here or won't come again. I'd like to have a look through the whole house. It's just possible that one room may hold their power more than others." He pushed his chair back and stood up. "Perhaps we could start with the bedrooms that were damaged?"

I led the way upstairs to my room, where the smashed Commodore was still on the desk. He cast his eyes over both computers, my bed, the cupboards, the wardrobes, and finally the curtains.

But all he said was, "It's a large bedroom."

"Yes, I believe it was the main bedroom at one time. The people who had the house before us extended one of the smaller ones over the utility room, and that's now the master bedroom with an en suite. Mum and Dad have that one."

"And that was damaged the other night too?"

"Yes, they all were, except Helen's."

As soon as we entered Sarah's room, the Reverend McBeil hurried over to several posters of pop stars that adorned her walls. Looking at the smiling faces of Paul Young and Simon Le Bon, he ran his hands over the glossy print. "Were these posters here when it happened?"

"Yes, they've been up for months."

"And they weren't damaged?"

"No. Nothing was really damaged in any of the rooms except for my computer. The sliding door of Mum's wardrobe was pulled off its runners, but it wasn't broken and slotted back in easily enough."

He stared hard at Sarah's posters. "I'd have thought if there'd been an evil entity here it would have homed in on these, for a start."

"Really? Why? They're just harmless posters, aren't they?"

"In the strictest sense of the word, yes. But the way teenagers tend to worship pop stars nowadays could be interpreted as paying homage to them and turning them into gods."

I vaguely remembered something from my Sunday school days in the dim and distant past. "Doesn't the Bible warn against false gods? I don't really understand what you mean, I'm afraid."

"The Holy Scriptures do indeed warn against false gods, which is exactly my point. The Bible tells us numerous times not to meddle with spirits because anything conjured up from another world is a servant of Satan, intent only on evil and misrule. So we have to ask whether these spirits would see pop stars, sporting heroes, and the like as a threat. With people, especially youngsters, worshipping such men and women as they do, don't you think Satan-spawn would focus their wrath on such false idols to prove their mistaken superiority, to try to persuade the young, gullible, and vulnerable to change their allegiance? It makes me wonder whether any creature from hell wouldn't simply attack an earthly idol of worship first, especially if it came across as a waxen, clay, or paper image."

The old boy had certainly thought his argument through to what he must have regarded as a logical conclusion, but which I regarded as merely old-fashioned.

"Can we move on to Helen's room now, please, Simon?"

"But hers wasn't damaged at all."

"Maybe not, but I'd still like to see it, please."

"Of course."

Closing Sarah's door behind us we walked around the bend in the landing to Helen's room. The first thing I saw when we went in was a saucepan on her bed. The second thing was the jewellery box Sarah bought her for her birthday. There was also the gold serpentine chain, a coat that Mum and Dad had promised her, a variety of new skirts and blouses, a couple more pieces of jewellery, and a key ring embossed with her name.

"The missing birthday presents," I gasped. "And the saucepan that disappeared from the kitchen a couple of days ago."

I turned to face the vicar who stood silently at the threshold, a disturbed look on his kindly features. His eyes were scanning every detail of the room, pausing now and again on the blue crushed velvet headboard, the window, and the presents arranged in neat rows on the bed itself.

"Something's been in here recently," he said starkly, taking several steps forward.

I shuddered visibly. "What do you mean, 'something'?"

He shook his head, a lock of white hair tumbling over his eyebrow. "I don't know yet. I don't think it's evil. . .it doesn't feel evil. I'm just getting a lingering sense of unhappiness and great loss. And yet there seems to be love, too."

Love! There was no love about the motherfucker that we'd been dealing with. Of that, I was totally sure.

"It isn't here now," he added slowly, "but it's been here not long ago. I sense both love and sorrow." The vicar's words were hesitant, as if he was unsure of how to express what he felt. "It's lingering in the room the same way perfume lingers."

I thought back to the expression of pure evil that I'd glimpsed on that face in my driving mirror. Whatever the vicar thought about our unwanted guest now, it was definitely fucking evil then, both in the car and in the sea at Brighton.

Evil didn't mix with love and sorrow, did it?

The Reverend McBeil was raising more questions than he was answering. I fingered Helen's presents, more concerned with how they got there than with something which he could only liken to perfume.

He appeared to latch on to my train of thought. "Helen wouldn't have put these here for some reason, would she?"

A flash of anger sparked into life. "Vicar, you're not suggesting that Helen is—?"

His raised hand cut my outburst short. "I'm not suggesting anything, my boy. I'm simply asking. These things got here somehow, didn't they?"

"Well, yes," I conceded. "But Helen wasn't even in the house when the saucepan disappeared. In fact, no one was except my mother and me. And you're surely not saying—?"

"I'm only asking. Nothing more. We need to look at every possibility."

"Even the possibility that someone in my family is lying about all this?" I asked with a touch of bitterness.

His response was immediate. "No. It's not that at all, as well you know." He put a hand on my shoulder. Then, without the harsh tone, "You're naturally upset at what's happening. No one's blaming you."

"But how did these things get here?"

"If we knew that we may be a little nearer to knowing why you need the services of—" He broke off and whirled round to face the door, his face swiftly draining of colour until it was a deathly grey.

"It's here," he whispered. "It's in the house."

I could sense nothing. But his words chilled me to the marrow. "What is it?" I hissed, afraid to speak in a normal tone.

"Shhh."

Everything was as it should be. Then I heard a faint clicking downstairs, followed by voices. Quiet and indistinct, but voices nonetheless.

The Reverend McBeil gripped my arm tightly. His fingers were as powerful as a vice. For one terrible second I relived the instant my wrists had been held underwater.

Gradually the voices became clearer, and I almost wept with relief.

"That's not a spirit, Vicar. It's Mark and Helen. They've been for a walk. We must have heard them coming in through the front door."

Breaking free of his grasp, I started towards the landing, but he caught my arm again.

"Simon, it's in this house," he insisted.

"It's Mark and Helen," I said, a little irritated. "I know their voices, Vicar." I could see by his eyes that he truly believed what he was saying, but I was sure the door opening had only accentuated the highly-charged atmosphere leading him to make a natural mistake.

"Come and meet them," I said, guiding him out of the room towards the stairs. As we descended, Mark and Helen approached along the hall.

"Good Lord!" exclaimed the vicar. He came to an abrupt halt four steps from the bottom. His chest heaved as his breathing accelerated and his lower lip shook. His eyes were wide and staring across to where Mark stood hand in hand with Helen.

I cleared the four steps in a single bound and reached for his hand. His body felt tight and rigid, and he seemed to be trying to say something, but the words came out in an unintelligible muddle.

"What's the matter with him?" called Mark.

"I don't know. He was fine a moment ago." I shook his arm gently and he appeared to regain a little of his composure. He broke his gaze from Mark, and as his eyes swivelled slowly toward me I noticed a tiny tic flickering just beneath his glasses. His trembling lip twisted into a semblance of a smile and he started scratching his head awkwardly.

"I I'm sorry," he stammered. "I just. . ." His eyes locked again on Mark and Helen. "I don't feel very well. Please excuse me." He stumbled past me, almost falling down the last four steps. As I caught his arm again to help him regain his balance, his hand closed over mine.

His eyes were pleading, almost wild. "Remember what I told you, Simon. Satan likes nothing more than to deal in lies and the make-believe. We must be wary of that which pretends to be the truth. We must not be emotional and draw the wrong conclusion. The real truth is that a sustained demonic attack is underway here. . ."

Demonic attack again. My inner voice had latched on to the vicar's phrase and wouldn't let it go.

". . .and my beliefs have taught me there are many ways of dealing with the truth. They give us a logical revelation and understanding of such happenings which defy other explanations."

Tearing my eyes from his agonised expression, I saw both Mark and Helen were staring at him dumbfounded. I knew how they felt.

"I'll contact my bishop this afternoon and be in touch with you to arrange an exorcism. In the meantime, for God's sake, be careful."

He broke into a trot down the hall, pausing at the front door before stepping through and pulling it shut behind him.

I stared at the closed door thoughtfully.

"What was all that about?" asked Mark.

"Search me. He was as right as rain until you two arrived."

Helen eyed me suspiciously. "What was he doing here, anyway?"

Now that was the crucial question and I was caught between a rock and a hard place thanks to Mark's lousy timing. The damning evidence in her bedroom meant there was no bluffing my way out. I would have to come clean.

I explained how we'd decided it would be best for the clergyman to look through the house to see if he felt we would benefit from an exorcism, but purposely left out all reference to yesterday's experiences. I kept one item of startling news to the end. "I don't know how they got there, but your birthday presents have turned up."

Their wide-eyed astonishment was obvious. "They've turned up in your bedroom," I continued. "The vicar and I found them while we were going over the house."

Helen was torn between surprise and fear. "But how. . .where've they been?"

I shrugged. "They were on your bed when I opened the door. That's all I know."

Fear got the better of her and she ran into the lounge, sobbing.

*　*　*

Dad was as stunned as everyone else when he got home from work that evening and we told him what had happened. He took Mark and me into the dining room, leaving Mum with Helen in the lounge.

"You might have told me what you were doing." He sounded angry that we'd gone behind his back.

"We only decided on the spur of the moment," I protested. "Things are getting too much for us now. We've got to get to the bottom of it. And quickly."

"I agree. But you should have told me before doing anything like that."

"You don't object, though, do you?"

"Of course I don't. And I'm glad you had the initiative to do it. But I'd still have appreciated being told what you were planning. I suppose now the vicar may do something about it?"

"Er, yes, he is," I said, hesitantly. "He's seeing the bishop with a view to getting permission to carry out an exorcism."

"What?" I thought Dad was going to explode. "Exorcising it! I thought that was something from the Dark Ages."

"Apparently not. From what the vicar tells me it's more common than people think." Whatever it was, it appeared to be creating its web around Helen, Mark, and me. But I felt it better if Dad thought it was affecting us all to the same degree. At least that way he couldn't let anything slip to Helen.

"I think we should all stay away from the house as much as possible until we can get everything sorted out," he said. "Mum's not started to cook dinner yet. We'll go out to eat tonight. It'll help keep our minds off what's going on."

Even without knowing the full facts, he realised we were facing a serious situation that could have dangerous consequences.

But at that moment he didn't know just how dangerous. And neither did I.

We were being forced to come to terms with a totally alien concept. Yet I felt, under the circumstances, to disbelieve the existence of the supernatural and the demonic would be more illogical than to believe. The time for detached intellectual rationalisation had passed. We needed to find the weapons to deal with these attacks.

Our principal weapon seemed to be the vicar.

CHAPTER 12: UNEARTHLY FIRE

THE FIRST THING I did upon waking from a deep sleep was to look at the clock. Quarter past four.

I'd eaten a vast amount of steak au poivre at the restaurant and fell asleep with a full stomach just moments after climbing into bed. Now I lay there for a few seconds, only half-registering what was going on outside my door.

Suddenly the noises snapped me into full consciousness and I distinguished a stampeding of feet on the landing accompanied by loud shouting and banging. Scrambling out of bed and pulling on my dressing gown, I stumbled into the passage just in time to see Dad disappearing into Mark's room.

A bright light flickered eerily through Mark's door and a rhythmic crackling filled the air. A mêlée of voices stormed rather than floated out to my ears, but it seemed as if everyone was shouting at once, destroying any sense the words may have had. When I saw through the doorway what was happening, a strangled gasp tore from my lips. Mum, Dad, and Helen were at Mark's bedside frantically beating at vivid orange flames that danced and leaped from the duvet. Beyond the fire, trapped by it, Mark cowered against the wall, trying to kick the blazing cover away.

Then I was aware of heavy breathing behind me.

"Sarah." I started to turn, expecting to see her frightened face.

No one was there. Instead, a faint shimmering and the hint of a dying laugh faded into the distance.

Then absolute stillness.

But there was no time to concern myself about things that weren't there. There was too much that *was* there. Mark was pinned in a corner by a semicircle of roaring fire. I looked about the room desperately for something with which to beat the ferocious flames.

Helen was screaming enough to wake the dead and her outstretched arms reached towards Mark who was still cowering behind the barrier of fire. The next moment Dad leaped across to the window and tugged with all his might at the curtains. They tore as he pulled them from the rail. I was beside him in a single bound and took one from him. Between us, we used them to batter the tongues of flame that licked menacingly towards Mark's shaking form. Time after time I hauled my curtain into the air, then whacked it down on the bed. The flames dipped each time but refused to die, springing back as I prepared for another blow.

The next second the fire was gone. It simply disappeared completely, as if it had never existed.

"What the hell's going on?" yelled Dad as he gazed horror-stricken at where the flames had been. They hadn't been put out by our efforts, but had just vanished.

Pressing himself against the wall, Mark looked as if he couldn't believe it either. A grim silence hit the room while everyone tried to take in what they had just seen. Then Helen started to sob, shattering the spell. She rushed over to the bed and, putting her arms around Mark's shoulders, eased him away from it.

I let out a sigh as I relaxed. It took a few seconds to register that the bedclothes were unmarked. There was no sign of scorching or burning anywhere. Dad noticed it too, and gingerly brushed his hand across the spot where the flames had been most ferocious. The blaze had been fierce and intense, yet left no damage in its wake.

Dad shot me an unnecessary glance; I had no intention of saying anything. Turning to Mum and Helen he said, "You'd better take Mark downstairs and give him a brandy. We'll be down in a moment."

"What do you make of this?" he asked when we were alone. I shook my head, the only answer I could give, and skirted my hand across the duvet.

"This is crazy," he said. "That fire was so fierce. And yet, now. . ." He gestured helplessly at the unmarked bedclothes.

I shivered involuntarily and for the first time thought about the temperature in the room. I could remember feeling the intense heat that had beaten us back from the flames. Now the atmosphere was chillingly cold.

"It was so real," I said. "At the time, anyway."

The ensuing silence mingled with the cold almost created a solid wall, unbreakable and unscaleable.

Then Dad was walking towards the door. "Let's see what Mark's got to say about it."

As I followed him out of the room I remarked casually, "Sarah must be sleeping like a log not to have heard anything." He stopped so abruptly I almost bumped into him.

Our thoughts became one. "Sarah!" we cried together.

While we ran towards her room I remembered how I'd expected to see her frightened face behind me a few moments earlier, but since then she'd slipped from my mind. A faint moaning came from beyond her door and on bursting in, I suffered my second major shock of the night. She was thrashing about wildly on the bed, with a pillow pressed tightly over her face. Both sides of the pillow were indented, as if held in place by two unseen hands. Dad grabbed the pillow.

"It won't move," he yelled, tugging with all his might. I grabbed it too. It resisted at first, then suddenly shot up and smothered me instead of Sarah. I stumbled off balance as it wrapped itself tightly over my nose and mouth, instantly cutting off my air supply.

No doubt my pleas for help were too muffled for Dad to understand what I was saying, but he got the general picture. I felt his strong hands gripping the pillow, trying to pull it off me. But I also felt pressure the other way. Someone, or something, was equally determined it should stay where it was.

My senses started to swim and I felt on the verge of passing out.

Desperately gasping for breath, I suddenly found I could breathe more freely again, and the pillow flopped limply in Dad's hands. The spinning walls began to slow down as my tortured lungs wheezed in huge gulps of air. Sarah's struggle for breath seemed easier now too.

Dad stood immediately beneath the ceiling light, his face shadowed, but I could still see a fierce glint in his eyes.

"That's enough," he said between clenched teeth. "We're not staying here another night until we get to the bottom of all this."

I coughed, pulling in another long breath of air and nodding at the same time. "I agree," I wheezed. "It's beyond a joke now." Suddenly I heard my inner voice speaking again. *It has been for some time.*

Dad helped us both downstairs where we joined everyone else in a stiff measure of brandy. For a while no one spoke. We were all too shaken by what had just happened, and became even more so when we told the others about the pillow.

Mum looked paler and more distraught than I'd ever seen. "It's tried to kill them, hasn't it Bob? It's tried to kill our children and Mark?"

"We're not spending another night here," he said firmly. "We're not going back to bed now, and first thing in the morning I'm booking us all into a hotel."

But would we be safe in a hotel? I wondered. *What about Brighton? What about the car?*

We spent the remainder of the night restlessly reading and dozing in our chairs. The first hint of daylight was beginning to creep in through the curtains when Sarah put a Paul Young CD on the stereo.

A thought suddenly struck me. "D'you know what?" I said, looking up sharply. "It's tomorrow already."

Realisation struck everyone at the same moment, and we followed Mark's lead in singing Happy Birthday and wishing Helen many happy returns.

If only we knew the horrors her birthday were going to bring us. Maybe it's as well that we didn't.

CHAPTER 13: THE PARTY

FROM WHERE WE SAT eating breakfast on our knees in the lounge we could hear Dad's voice in the hall. "That's fine then, Harry," he was saying into the telephone. "I don't know what time we'll be over, though. Are you sure you don't mind waiting up for us? Thanks, Harry. Appreciate it. See you later."

He came into the lounge just as Mum brought his muesli and toast on a tray. "That's all fixed," he said, taking the tray. "Harry's got rooms for us all at the Grenadier, and says he doesn't mind what time we get over there after the party. By the way, Helen, he says 'Happy Birthday' to you."

Helen smiled at the thought of jocular Harry Milburn, the landlord of Meriton's solitary hotel. It was the first smile I'd seen since our own greeting to her four hours ago.

By nine thirty, three men arrived to put up the marquee, and the drinks arrived by van from the village off-licence twenty minutes later.

With all the activity around us, and the sun rising rapidly in a cloudless sky, the horrors of the previous night, and indeed the whole mysterious happenings of the past few days, dissolved away like an ice cube left out in the midday heat.

Happiness and expectation buzzed everywhere I looked. The garden, already beginning to take on colour from the early summer bedding plants, quickly assumed a gaudy mask of red, blue, yellow, and white as we fastened balloons and streamers to tree branches and windows. By lunchtime it looked like the scene of a village fête, but there was still much to be done, so we made do with snatching a couple of sandwiches between stringing fairy lights above the lawn and setting the drinks up at the cooled bar that Dad had hired.

Despite our protests, Helen insisted on helping, donning tatty jeans and a T-shirt. "This is my party," she said. "I'm going to make sure everything's done right."

The disc jockey arrived at three in the afternoon with a van load of electronic gadgetry, vinyl records, and CDs. I helped him unravel miles of cable from what he called his "DJ talk unit," which we took to the power point in the garage. There were half a dozen speakers and a variety of flashing coloured lights to be wired up and connected to the talk unit, which comprised twin record decks, a CD player, mixer, and microphone.

Mark shinned up a ladder to place speakers atop trees all around the garden, and everything eventually began to fall into place. The hammers and nails were whisked away out of sight, cables were made as unobtrusive as possible, the pump used for inflating the balloons was fixed back onto Dad's old bike in the garage, and blown bulbs in the fairy lights had been replaced. Dad sampled the beer—"Just to make sure it's alright," he said—and the DJ blasted our ears with a few bars of "Rock Around The Clock."

Soon the DJ blew into the microphone a couple of times. "One two, testing, one two, one two, testing. This is Rod Roll the Rocker. Testing, testing."

"Is that really his name?" grinned Mark.

"His stage name, yes."

"You idiot." He playfully thumped me on the arm. "I hardly thought it was his real name."

I grinned back. "He's quite good too. Plays some decent stuff. Plenty of modern ones and some good old rock 'n' rollers. He DJed a party I went to last Christmas."

The caterers arrived at four and Mum supervised while they were getting the sandwiches, sausage rolls, vol-au-vents, cold roast beef, pork and lamb, salad, cakes, and fruit set up on trestle tables in the marquee.

As time drew on, Helen went in to change, so again Mark and I found a quiet minute to ourselves and decided to double-check Dad's opinion of the beer.

"It's really good of your Dad to fork out for the party. I had to wait for my twenty-first before I had anything like this."

"We tend to mark the decades, rather than the more commercialised anniversaries. And Helen said she'd rather have a big do for her twentieth, in keeping with that tradition."

"She won't be having a biggie like this next year, then?"

"No. This one's in lieu, so to speak."

"The beer's not bad," said Mark, eyeing his now empty glass. "I'd not realised I'd downed my pint so quickly. Are you sure you've not been having a swig of my ale?"

"Quite sure," I grinned, reaching under the table for my own pint pot.

"Look, this has got to go down well, for Helen's sake," said Mark softly. "Whatever this thing is that's haunting you, it mustn't spoil her big day. Between us we mustn't let her out of our sight all night, okay?"

I nodded. "Agreed. I'll pop up and get changed. See you soon."

It took much longer to daub on the aftershave and comb my hair than it did to actually dress, and it was a good hour before I was ready to go downstairs again. A last look in the mirror and I was good to go. *Yes*, I thought, *not bad*. I had my eye on one or two of Helen's friends, and I thought that I wouldn't have any trouble pulling looking like the way I did.

A final quick flick to ensure any errant hairs were firmly in their place and I made my way back to the lawn.

Helen had already changed and was cuddling up to her boyfriend on a bench at the far side of the garden. She looked stunning in her chosen party attire: a simple knee-length black panne dress and bare feet.

I strolled towards them. "Hi, lovebirds. Let me look after your date, Mark, while you exchange those tattered trousers and grubby shirt for something just a touch more becoming."

He jumped up. "I thought you'd never offer." He disappeared towards the house and I nestled down in his place beside my sister.

She appeared tense. "I hope everything's going to be alright tonight."

"Of course it is," I said, hoping I looked and sounded more confident than I felt. "I'll look after things for you."

"It's just that after the last few days. . ." She shrugged, leaving the rest unsaid.

It was quarter of an hour later when the loudspeaker above our heads suddenly burst into life. "A very good evening to you, lads and lasses, and welcome to the Rod Roll the Rocker special birthday extravaganza! Before we get things really moving, let's say one very big happy birthday to our hostess tonight, the very lovely Helen Reynolds. Happy birthday, sweetheart, and many more of them. I'll be giving you a mention every hour on the hour tonight, just in case your guests forget why they're here. But in the meantime, here's a little number from Sade to get us in the mood."

The music, which had been fading up slowly under his voice, blasted to a crescendo. The party was underway.

And what a party it was.

Somehow, all eighty-five guests managed to find space to dance, eat, and drink. The music was loud and cheerful, so was the DJ, and so, it appeared, was Helen. A couple of trestle tables pushed together at one side of the lawn were now overflowing with presents left there by her friends. I was pleased to see her wearing the gold serpentine necklace I'd given her, and a gold gate bracelet from Mark adorned her right wrist.

Overhead, the fairy lights shone and the disco lights flashed their unremitting beat in time to the music, casting shades of green, red, yellow, and blue over the contorting bodies on the lawn. Another blaze of flashing colour snaked around the disco centre itself in the form of ten separate pieces of linear rope lights, each about eight metres long. The high-powered voices of Elton John and Millie Jackson pounding out their "Act of War" sent the lights into an apoplectic frenzy, and the writhing dancers on the grass stepped up a gear, bobbing and swaying rhythmically in quick tempo.

I scanned the throng, looking for just one tiny sign that anything was amiss. Nothing. Everything seemed perfect. Yet something at the back of my mind told me that it was lurking, unseen, awaiting its chance.

I was sure that it was unabashed that eighty-five people were present, and was watching and getting ready to make its nightly appearance. And what would it do this time? No one would see it if it simply made its usual dash past the window; they were too busy dancing, eating, drinking, enjoying themselves.

So what if it became the growing thing again and filled the air above the lawn with its foul, evil presence, as it had done to me once before? Was that its scheme? Was that what it was waiting to do?

Happy, smiling faces surrounded me, making the events of the last few days seem far away and so unreal. The party seemed to be blocking out the nameless terror that had plagued us. I knew normality was fragile; all it needed was a split second. But the party was helping us forget.

Titus was enjoying himself as much as anyone. He loved noise and activity, but above all he loved the fuss and attention everyone was foisting upon him. By nature, he was gregarious and outgoing, and if anyone as much as stroked him he became their firm friend for life. I saw him make at least fifty new friends in just half an hour. He trotted happily around the edge of the lawn looking at the dancers but decided finally not to join in himself. Eventually he set up camp just outside the marquee where he waylaid guests as they came out with plates of food, managing to scrounge a morsel of meat or pie from almost everyone who fell prey to his huge brown eyes.

"Act of War" faded down thirty seconds before its end to let Rod Roll the Rocker's frenzied voice burst through the speakers. "And there we have Elton John and Millie Jackson signing a peace treaty across the waters. Time, in a moment, for another blast from the past with the evergreen Rolling Stones and "Jumpin' Jack Flash" going all the way back to '68. But right now it's a shade after nine, and that can mean only one thing. . ."

From where I stood a couple of metres from the disco unit I saw him release the second turntable to unleash a double-speed version of "Happy Birthday," while he quickly swapped "Act of War" for "Jumpin' Jack Flash." In a few seconds it was cued up, and as "Happy Birthday" died away leaving the revellers still trying to keep pace, the night became awash with the Rolling Stones.

A couple of dancers broke away from the pack and headed towards me. It was Sarah, hanging on to Steve's arm. She had chosen tight-fitting, black ski pants with stirrups, and, like her sister, had opted for bare feet. Even though it was a hot night, she wore her thick double-breasted cerise jacket over a thin black shirt. Steve, with a couple of blond streaks running through his dark brown hair and a short sleeve, tie-dyed khaki shirt tucked into the waistband of his grey zip leg-pocket jeans, oozed the street hero rebel.

"Hi," breathed Sarah, pulling away from her boyfriend and flopping her arms across my shoulder. "We're off to get some food. Are you coming?"

I nodded enthusiastically. Although I had already made several trips to the marquee I felt it was time for another.

Dusk was beginning to steal the sun, and a couple of arc lights fastened to a horizontal bar inside the marquee had been switched on; their intense white light made the interior as bright as day.

Mum was in charge of the food while Dad kept watch over the bar. He caught my eye and beckoned me to join him. Cupping my hands, I shouted above the noise to Sarah, "I'm going to have a word with Dad. I'll join you later."

I made my way behind the bar and Dad moved alongside me. "How's it going out there?" he asked.

"Fine. Everyone seems to be enjoying themselves."

"And Helen?"

"Especially Helen. The last time I saw her she was going off to dance with Mark. He's not let her out of his sight all night."

"Have you seen anything of our unwanted guest?"

"No. And I'm hoping if it wanted to make its presence known it would have by now." Although my mind was fixed firmly again on the memory of that half-glimpsed vicious, hateful face that had appeared in the car mirror and the underwater encounter, I tried to be confident and hopeful. "I'll have another beer, please," I said, more jauntily than I felt.

More thoughts sprang up as I wandered away towards the trestles of food. Was the thing a potential killer or was it simply trying to warn us of something? I mulled over the possibilities. After it flung me away from Mark in the sea it didn't attack again, neither did it call on more power after I broke its spell in the car. Although we hadn't known it at the time, the flames on Mark's bed were harmless. But what would have happened to Sarah if Dad and I hadn't found that pillow fastened over her face? I shuddered at the vivid recollection of choking while the pillow smothered me.

Thankfully, my thoughts were interrupted by a pair of arms flung around my neck, which almost made me spill my beer in surprise.

I looked into the smiling face of Janice Briggs hovering only inches from mine. "Come on Simon," she purred. "You promised me a dance, remember?"

Oh, don't worry, there was no way I would forget that. The fact that she was an active member of the bring-back-the-mini-skirt brigade ensured she would linger in my memory.

"Hang on," I said, quaffing my pint in one go.

Her three-inch heels pierced the grass as soon as she led the way out of the marquee and stepped off the canvas floor onto the lawn. She slipped off her shoes and made her way towards the dancing. I looked at her rear, appreciatively, and couldn't help but wonder whether the hem of her pure white cotton skirt was nearer to her chin than her ankles. I wouldn't have liked to lay odds on it either way. Her red cotton jersey halter top was knotted at the front, exposing her midriff. Short raven hair tapered at the base of her neck, around which was slung a black necklace comprising large Perspex lumps, and her pierced ears each sported two red hoops.

She made her way to a bench and slid her shoes under the seat, then ran barefoot to the edge of the dancers where she turned and waited for me to catch up before pulling me into the throng.

The record on the turntable was not one I recognised but needed a fairly active step to keep in time. Ignoring that fact, Janice linked her arms behind my neck and started squirming sideways in a style more suited to a smoochy number.

Janice Briggs was sixteen and had just left school. Her father ran the village hardware shop and she was going to begin working behind the counter there full time. I guessed that trade would soon be boosted by a stream of Meriton's boys popping in for a packet of nails, a ball of twine, and a chat. She was certainly a very attractive girl from whichever angle you viewed her.

The smell of herbal shampoo wafted up from her shining hair and mixed with a none-too-delicate perfume giving the impression that she had bathed in it rather than dabbed it on.

After a couple more dances, during which she kept her arms firmly entwined around my neck, I managed to untangle myself and led her back to the bench where she had left her shoes. She sat down rather heavily, again draping her long willowy arms across my shoulders, and pulled my lips onto hers. Mechanically, I submitted to her kiss, but only half-heartedly returned it. I was aware of her tongue probing my mouth while her fingers twirled locks of my hair. Although my arms were around her waist, it could hardly be said that I was holding her. It was more by accident than design that my linked fingers rested on the bare flesh of her back between her shirt and her skirt.

Her own fingers moved back from my shoulders, and made their way down my chest to my growing bulge. Slowly she began rubbing the front of my trousers, taking obvious delight as the swelling increased under her gentle touch. Gripping tighter, her tenderness disappeared. I squirmed slightly, trying to control my emotions.

Was this right with so many eyes around, including Mum and Dad's and, possibly, our nemesis? That final thought spurred me into action. Despite the continued stirrings of my manhood, I gently eased her hand away.

Suddenly she pushed me back and jumped up, her dark eyes flashing accusingly. "What's the matter with you? Don't you want me?"

"Sorry? I don't know what—"

"I've had a better reaction from litmus paper. What's bugging you? Is there someone else here tonight that you like better than me?"

"Er. . .no. No, there's no one else, Janice. You know I like you."

"It seems like it." Sarcasm twisted her words and made them ugly, almost to the point of bitterness.

"It's just that there's. . .look, I'm sorry. Come on, sit down." I smiled into those suspicious eyes and watched with satisfaction as they melted into the warmth they had shown earlier.

She sat back down. Her hand reached for my still-bulging crotch. I moaned at the touch, and—

Suddenly a blood-curdling howl pierced the night as the music stopped and the lights dimmed. Instinctively Janice squeezed with a vice-like grip, then scrambled up. I leaped off the bench and looked towards the dancers. The overhead fairy lights were still on, but the disco lights had gone off, and so had the linear rope lights.

In the immediate aftermath of the scream, a deathly silence and stillness descended on the party. One moment the dancers were twisting and weaving about the grass; the next they were immobile, rooted to the spot. Then the world came alive again, starting with a murmur from the disco revellers and then swiftly growing to shouts and then screams.

"What's happened?" I yelled, frantically sprinting towards them. Mass hysteria was sweeping Helen's guests.

"What's happened?" I cried again. One ashen-faced youth stood apart from the rest. I gripped him by the shoulders, but his eyes stared back at me blankly. I shook him fiercely; he felt like a rag doll. Then, beyond him, I saw the cause of it all.

Rod Roll the Rocker was scrambling up from the shrubs behind and a little to the side of his disco unit. A violent crackling filled the air as blue sparks showered in a small fountain across the controls. Two shapes were sprawled on the grass and alongside them stood Helen screaming hysterically, her head shaking wildly and her bloodless lips drawn back as tight as they could go.

Frantically I swung my horrified gaze away from the still forms on the ground to Helen and back again. It was only then that one of the two figures registered in my mind as having four legs, one of which twitched uncontrollably, as if responding to the pull of a mad puppet master. It was Titus. And next to him, recognisable now from the unmoving profile, was Mark. Running through Titus's mouth was the electric cable connecting the disco equipment to the mains supply in the garage, and Mark's left hand was gripping the dog's head firmly.

I started forward but someone grabbed my shoulder, spinning me round. "No. Don't touch him. He's had an electric shock."

"We've got to get them," I insisted, not really understanding what I was doing. This didn't seem to be me. I was somewhere else, refusing to take all this in.

"Where's the power supply?" It was the same youth who had stopped me touching Mark.

"In the garage," I managed to stammer, trying to break free from his grasp.

"Don't touch them," he repeated urgently. "Not until the power's off."

Vaguely I saw someone sprint across the lawn towards the garage door.

I didn't want to believe what was happening. Somehow, Janice's overpowering perfume and wonderfully exquisite grip on my manhood had made me delirious. Any moment now, I would wake up to a wet sticky mess in my pants.

Fuck, yes.

"Don't touch the machine." Again, words of warning hammered through my numbness. Rod Roll the Rocker had reached out to within an inch of the disco controls, but now stood frozen on hearing the urgency of the command aimed at him.

I seemed to be detached, witnessing the scene from a great distance, only half seeing another figure haul the DJ away from the still sparking turntables.

Then Dad's voice from behind me, close, yet a million miles away. I had no idea what he was saying. I looked at him helplessly, then turned away, tears in my eyes.

Mark and Titus lay unmoving on the grass. Titus's twitching leg stilled now.

"Not yet, Mr. Reynolds." This time it was Dad who had to be held back. All of a sudden the crackling stopped and the fountain of sparks died.

"Okay." A voice from the garage. "The power's off."

As I watched, dumbstruck, several people descended on Mark and Titus. Someone pulled the chewed and frayed cable away from the dog's mouth. I was still in a daze but Dad, who seemed to be in full control, pushed through, dropping to his knees beside Mark, pressing his right ear to the unmoving chest.

"Simon," yelled Dad. "Stop daydreaming and see to Helen."

His harsh tone snapped me back to reality. I would not be waking to an empty, spent manhood. This reality was more fucked up than that.

Focusing again, I realised exactly what was happening. Helen was still screaming hysterically and her guests crowded around to see why. As soon as I clasped her to me, the torrent of sound was silenced, replaced by a flood of tears.

"He's dead, Simon," she sobbed. "He's dead. I know he is."

I squeezed her tightly, trying to comfort her as best I could, while Dad felt for a pulse in Mark's neck. He looked up sharply, as if a thought had suddenly struck him.

"Has anyone phoned an ambulance?" he shouted. "Tell them his heart's stopped. And for God's sake, hurry."

Turning his attention back to Mark, he landed a heavy blow on the breastbone. A couple of Helen's friends disappeared towards the house while Dad gripped Mark's nose. Then he placed his mouth over Mark's and blew steadily. It seemed an eternity before the air forced into Mark's lungs caused his chest to rise; it fell limply as soon as Dad backed off.

Dad's face was ashen as he lowered his mouth over Mark's again.

"Oh, God," sobbed Helen, burying her head deep in my shoulder.

Sleep, sleep, sleep. That inner voice again. The same mocking voice I heard in the car that lulled me to sleep on the way back from Brighton. All control suddenly seemed to flee from me.

"Who are you?" I screamed at the top of my voice. "What do you want from us? Why don't you leave us alone?"

I was aware of all eyes swivelling from Dad's frantic life-saving bid to me. They must have thought I was crazy, but at that precise moment I didn't give a flying fuck whether they did or not. Nor, indeed, whether I really was crazy. All I cared about, in an intense and sudden blaze of passion, was my family and Mark. I'd had enough of this being from hell tormenting us. I wanted it gone. I wanted the vicar to destroy it.

But first, Mark's heart.

Dad ran his hand along Mark's chest locating the sternum. He pushed sharply, rocked back, pushed again, rocked back, again and again and again. Interspersed with mouth-to-mouth resuscitation, he kept up the relentless blows on Mark's chest seemingly for hours, but in this fucked up reality it was merely a matter of moments before he shouted triumphantly, "His heart's started."

Only then did Dad allow himself to sink back wearily onto the grass. Mum had been alongside him, watching the life-giving process through widened, terrified eyes. Now that Mark was breathing, she gently eased Helen away from me and led her, still sobbing, towards the house.

I didn't need to examine Titus to know our beloved pet was dead. Helplessly, I turned to the DJ. "What happened?" I asked in tones so quiet I could barely hear them myself.

"I don't know," said Rod. "Someone suddenly shouted and the next thing there was a tremendous bang and I was blown off my seat."

A couple of teenagers stepped forward. "Titus was lying by the disco asleep, I think," said one of them. "All at once he leaped up and stared towards the house, growling. I couldn't see anything to upset him, but he'd certainly got his eye on something."

I groaned inwardly. In my heart of hearts, I already knew what had caused this mayhem.

"Then he howled and cowered up against the unit," the boy continued, pointing towards the disco's control box. "He barked then ran round the side and started to bite the cable."

The youth paused momentarily and cocked his head in Mark's direction, who was still lying unconscious on the ground but breathing evenly. "That chap tried to stop him, but the dog wouldn't let go of the cable. Then there was a bang and sparks everywhere."

"That's hardly surprising," said Rod, peering down at the cable. About a metre away from the unit, the cable's white PVC coating was torn away, revealing the wires inside. Poor Titus's teeth had gone straight through those as well. Shreds of copper glinted in the fading light. The electricity had surged through Titus into Mark.

I felt myself becoming detached as my mind wandered back to the thought of Titus growling at something unseen. I hardly noticed the ambulance crew rushing through the garden to lift Mark onto a stretcher. Dad's voice sounded distant and remote when he told me that Mum, Sarah, and Helen were going to the hospital and he and I would stay behind to clear things away.

The guests started to drift away as soon as the ambulance siren faded on its way to Merebrook Royal Infirmary nine miles away.

Almost like a robot, I went through the motions of fetching speakers from their vantage points all around the garden and helping the DJ wind seemingly endless miles of cable around its reel. All the time I tried to imagine the scene inside the ambulance. Mark would be strapped on a stretcher to one side of the central aisle with an oxygen mask clamped over his nose and mouth while a paramedic sat nearby ensuring he was still alive. Mum, Helen, and Sarah would be huddling up to each other on the opposite side of the vehicle, with the driver radioing ahead to warn the hospital an emergency was on its way in.

Not once did I look at my watch while we worked to return some semblance of order to the garden. We closed Titus's staring eyes and covered his limp body with a blanket.

Eventually Dad shut the front door, cutting the noise of the DJ's minibus as it crunched down the gravel drive.

"How could that happen?" he muttered, leading the way to the lounge.

I told him what the two teenagers saw. He covered his eyes, slowly running both palms down his face.

Minutes passed in silence.

"We're all going to church tomorrow," he announced suddenly, sitting bolt upright and downing a double measure of brandy in one swallow. "We're going to get the vicar to carry out this exorcism thing straight away."

"He did say something about seeing his bishop. . ."

"We're not setting foot in this house again until he's done it. We've got the rooms at the Grenadier. We'll stay there until it's all over."

I thought of poor Titus, lying cold and still under the blanket. The sight of the terrible scorch marks on the fur around his mouth would stay with me for a very long time. The memory was interrupted by the telephone bell.

It was Mum. Mark was going to be fine. "He's come round and says he's hungry," she told me. "His hand's badly burned where he tried to get the cable out of Titus's mouth." I could hear her choking back tears at the mention of Titus's name. "He took quite a jolt. The doctors say he's lucky to be alive. It seems Titus took the brunt of it."

"How's Helen?"

"They've given her something to calm her down. She's better now that she knows Mark's going to be alright."

"When are you coming home?"

"Anytime now. They're keeping Mark in until Monday for observation. They want to make sure there aren't any complications. There's nothing more we can do here, so we'll be leaving shortly. We'll get a taxi."

"They're getting a taxi," I mouthed to Dad.

He indicated that he wanted to speak to her. He told Mum we'd pack a few things for them and that we'd all be spending the night at the hotel.

"We'll pick you up from the hospital in about an hour," he said. "There's only one more job left to do here."

What a job it was. We buried Titus at the side of the lawn in the spot where he loved to play. It took considerably longer than we thought; it was over two hours before we arrived at the hospital.

CHAPTER 14: PREPARATION

"OH GOD our help in ages past, our hope for years to come. . ." My own tuneless singing in church the next morning helped swell the powerful hymn of praise, although, for what must have been the thousandth time in a few short days, my mind wasn't on what I was doing but instead was pondering over the trouble we found ourselves in. We had been driven from our home, unable to return for fear of what would befall us next, and were pinning our hopes on one man—the elderly vicar who now stood before us in the pulpit leading his congregation at worship.

It wasn't a large gathering—no more than thirty, including Mum and Dad, Sarah, Helen, and myself—and it seemed the vicar could hardly take his eyes off our family throughout the service. He caught sight of us as soon as he stepped out of the vestry and a troubled look played over his face. His attention appeared to be taken with Helen more than anyone else, but I noticed that during one verse of the first hymn he fixed me with a constant stare.

It was years since I had been in a church, but it was just as I remembered: the great stone walls were just as cold, the ceiling just as high, and the stained glass windows just as majestic. A deep red cloth depicting a shining golden crucifix was draped over the altar, on which stood a large wooden cross flanked by silver candlesticks. At the side of the solitary shallow step that separated the nave from the chancel, a set of winding stairs led up to the pulpit. The choir stalls were behind the pulpit, and the organ stood on a raised platform opposite.

After almost an hour the service was drawing to a close and my mind slipped back to the matter in hand as the vicar closed his prayer book.

"May the love of God and the fellowship of the Holy Spirit be with us all now and forever more. Amen."

The rich mellow tones of the ancient organ erupted through their pipes while the vicar stepped down and walked past us towards the main door.

I was sitting by the aisle and was about to get up. "Not yet," Dad hissed from the other end of the family group. "Wait until everyone's out, then we can get the vicar to ourselves for a few moments."

A couple of minutes later we stepped out into the bright sunshine to where the vicar stood by the porch.

"I'm very pleased to see you, Mr. Reynolds," he said, shaking Dad's outstretched hand. "And the whole family too." He paused, looking at us all in turn. "Something's happened, hasn't it?"

"I'm afraid it's much worse than when you last spoke to Simon," Dad told him. He swiftly recounted the events at Helen's party last night.

"Dear, oh dear," exclaimed the Reverend McBeil at the end of the story. "Things are more developed than I feared. I'm seeing the Bishop tomorrow to discuss our next step. I'll be recommending that he give me the go-ahead to carry out an exorcism."

"We're not going back to that house until something's done to get rid of whatever's there," insisted Dad.

"Quite right, very wise," agreed the vicar. "An exorcism will cleanse your home of whatever evil spirit is there."

"What does it involve?"

"Put simply, Mr. Reynolds, it's a means of expelling a spirit from a person or place."

"What do you have to do?"

"It's a series of prayers, adjurations, and rites. It's not a complicated procedure at all."

"How long does it take?" Dad asked.

"It depends on how firmly entrenched the spirit is in your home and how hostile it is. It could be over in a matter of minutes, or it could take hours—even days. There's no way of telling until we begin."

I saw Mum pale at the thought of it taking days.

"Why do you need to speak to the Bishop?" Dad asked. "Can't you just do it today? Now?"

"It is possible, but it would be going against church policy. I think it'd be better to leave it until—"

"Dad," I blurted out suddenly. "That pillow wasn't the first time it's tried to kill us. When Mark and Helen and I went to Brighton it tried to drown Mark and almost caused us to crash on the way home."

Helen stared at me in disbelief. "Simon," she gasped, "what's this all about? You said Mark got cramp."

Dad listened tight-lipped as I told him the truth about our day at the seaside.

"It definitely means you harm," said the vicar when I finished. "There's no doubt about that. Look, I want you all to stay for lunch and tea at the vicarage, and after tonight's service I'll go with you to White Pastures and carry out the exorcism."

"I need to go home and tidy up," Mum began, but the Reverend McBeil raised his hands. "There is acute danger at White Pastures, that's been proven. And from what Simon's told us about Brighton and your car, you're not safe from it anywhere. The best place I can think for you to be is here."

* * *

"We might be nearing the end of the twentieth century," said the vicar over an excellent lunch of piping hot roast beef (cooked rare, just the way I liked it), Yorkshire pudding, boiled potatoes, peas, and carrots that Mrs. Jackson managed to conjure up for us all, "but the occult is still very much with us."

"Do you mean evil spirits regularly take over people's homes?" Mum asked him.

The vicar smiled. "Hardly what I'd call regularly, but it does happen more often than people might think."

"I thought spirits and exorcisms were straight from the Dark Ages, or the fertile imagination of filmmakers," said Dad.

"Far from it, Mr. Reynolds. Evil spirits pose a very real and serious threat. And don't forget that for some, witchcraft—the art of black magic and summoning spirits—is just part of everyday life. A spirit often comes to take possession of a person to bend them to the will of Satan, but in many cases it's been brought about by meddling with the occult."

"We've never practiced black magic. We've never even as much as played with a Ouija board or called up spirits in any way," my father protested. "So why should we be haunted? What's causing it?"

Again the vicar smiled. "I wish I knew, Mr. Reynolds. Houses can be haunted for any number of reasons, most commonly perhaps by a spirit that isn't inherently evil or malicious, but can't move on into the next world until it's righted some wrong on earth. As a Christian and an active member of the church, I believe passionately in the resurrection and the day of judgement. Man shall live again and dwell in the house of the Lord for all eternity. The mercy of God is infinite and His power over this earthly realm is awesome. But there's another whose power is just as strong—the devil, Satan, Prince Lucifer. Whatever you want to call him, he's the same being. He dwells in his own abode beyond the gates of hell and is forever on the lookout for souls he can entrap into serving him."

"But you don't think this thing that's haunting us is from hell do you?" asked Dad. "After all, you did tell Simon you could sense love and sorrow in the house."

"And so I did. But it wasn't love that held young Mark Brody underwater. It wasn't love that almost sent Simon to sleep in a bid to make your car crash. It wasn't love that sent flames to Mark's bedroom. It wasn't love that tried to suffocate two of your children. And it wasn't love that killed your dog."

"Are you sure it was love you felt?"

"Without a doubt. But I also felt sorrow and a certain amount of resentment."

"Resentment?"

The vicar narrowed his eyes, seemingly unsure for a moment as to how to continue. "I say resentment, but perhaps that's the wrong word for it. Not jealousy, either. More like confusion, really. But love was certainly the overpowering emotion it left behind."

Helen put down her knife and fork. "What can it want, though?"

"We may never know," the vicar answered, softly. "We're certainly not going to ask it."

"Just what are we going to do?" Dad wanted to know.

"We're going to pray for you to be released from your burden, and we're also going to pray for the soul of whatever is waiting for us in the shadows at White Pastures."

"Pray for that murderous thing?" snapped Dad.

"I'm convinced it's not altogether evil. It may be a fledgling and confused servant of Lucifer struggling to understand what it's being asked to do. It's certainly done you mischief, but—"

"Mischief! Come off it, Vicar. That's an understatement. It killed our dog and attacked my children and their friends!"

"There's no doubt it means you harm, but if it were inherently evil it wouldn't have left love in its wake."

"Well I've certainly never felt love when it's been around."

"It's love of an intangible kind. A spiritual, eternal love. Perhaps that's something you're not entirely familiar with, Mr. Reynolds."

"You mean because I'm not a churchgoer?"

"I didn't say that. What I want to do is to make you see the importance of praying for your own salvation and for the salvation of the spirit so it can find sufficient release and happiness of its own, so that it leaves you alone."

"What if it can't find its own release?"

"When we get to the house and begin the exorcism I believe that whatever's troubling you won't be able to resist a Christian order of banishment given in the name of God the Father and Jesus Christ his Son."

For the first time I began to feel as if we were finally seeing light at the end of the long, dark tunnel. "You're saying, then, that our troubles could be over tonight?"

"I sincerely hope so, Simon. But we need to prepare ourselves first. Straight after lunch I want you all to go back to the church and pray for God's help and guidance."

"And just how do we do that?" my dad asked.

"You can be sure, Mr. Reynolds, that God already knows of your problems. You must ask him to help you now, in your time of need, by sheltering you from harm, in particular from evil influences that may strive to overcome you during the task which lies ahead."

By two thirty we were back in the cold pews.

"I will open your prayers," said the Reverend McBeil. "Then I'll leave you to pray in your own way."

Dad looked up sharply. "I've not prayed for years. What guarantee is there that your God will even listen to us?"

The Reverend McBeil smiled indulgently. "He's not just my God. He's yours too, if you did but know it, and he will listen to your prayers." He climbed the pulpit steps and looked down on us kneeling below him.

"Dear Lord, have mercy on the souls of Robert Reynolds and his family in this, their hour of need. Keep them safe and whole, and give them strength to do your bidding against a servant of Lucifer. Keep their minds clear for the task they face, and their resolve firm and steadfast. We ask this in the name of God the Father, God the Son and God the Holy Ghost. Amen."

He stepped down from the pulpit and touched my shoulder as he passed. "Pray yourselves now. Silent prayer if you wish. It is just as powerful." He moved down the aisle slowly, towards the door.

No one spoke. I looked along the line of bowed heads, wondering where to begin.

Oh Lord, help us, please, I said to myself. *Guide and protect us and make us emerge victorious.* Once I'd started it seemed easier to keep up the flow, but every so often my phrases returned to pleas for help. Gradually I began to feel less tense, and a calm, inner peace settled upon me. Somehow I found the words to continue my silent prayer until the vicar returned in just over half an hour.

A few hours later we were seated at those same pews again for the evening service. There were a few more faces than there had been in the morning, and they were all people I knew by sight from the village.

Throughout the service I constantly glanced at my watch, willing time to speed up. Eventually the vicar brought the service to a halt, and we trooped back to the vicarage where he disappeared upstairs. He returned ten minutes later still wearing his black ankle-length robe and carrying a large plastic bag.

"A Bible, some candles, and other things we may need," he explained.

The Reverend McBeil got into the passenger seat of Dad's Rover while Mum, Helen, Sarah, and I squeezed together in the back. Everyone was solemn as Dad clicked the automatic transmission into drive and we purred out onto the road for the short journey to our home.

"Now remember," said the vicar, turning to peer into the back, "prayer is one of the most powerful forces in the world. We have prepared well for our battle tonight, and I have every confidence."

The rest of the two-mile journey was spent in silence. Dad slowed the car to a crawling pace as he swung it through the double gates onto the gravel drive. The tyres crunched slowly over the tiny stones. It was 8:50 p.m. when we stopped outside the oak front door.

Our home appeared to have undergone a tangible change. The usually cheerful place that radiated friendliness from the white pebble-dashed walls now looked gaunt and forlorn, with a hint of grimness in the façade. It was no longer the happy place we'd made it over the last four years, but had degenerated into an inhospitable shell, inhabited by an unwanted being from another plane of life.

But only temporarily, I said to myself. *Whatever you are, your days are numbered. We've come to reclaim White Pastures. You're going back where you belong.*

I felt Helen shudder alongside me as she, no doubt, recalled memories of her party and its tragic end just twenty-four hours earlier.

We stood for a few seconds and simply stared up at the windows. The air felt thick and humid, full of a clammy stickiness that threatened to engulf us. The sun had dropped behind the trees at the bottom of the garden and a hazy orange glow washed over the lower part of the sky. A cat appeared briefly on the wall separating the northern edge of the garden from the lane leading to the village. It scampered to within a few metres of the house when suddenly its hackles rose and, spitting once amidst a hissing and flurry of fur, it darted away and vanished from sight.

There was no movement behind those panes of glass. Just a dark, still emptiness looking out, mocking, inviting, almost daring us to enter its domain and face whatever lay within.

As Dad slotted his key into the lock and the heavy oak door swung open, I noticed the Reverend McBeil shuffle through the contents of his plastic bag before letting it dangle from his wrist by its handle.

As I moved towards the door and braced myself to go inside I felt my heart thump, pushing adrenalin wildly through my bloodstream. Plucking up every ounce of my waning courage, I stepped over the threshold.

CHAPTER 15: CONFRONTATION

DESPITE HIS ADVANCING YEARS the vicar was a powerful and imposing figure in his black cassock, holding a candle in one hand and a Bible in the other. He seemed even taller once inside the house, almost as if he had grown in stature to combat whatever lay ahead.

"I'll begin in the hall at the foot of the stairs. That's the centre, the connecting point of the whole house," he said. "The power I summon will find the spirit from there, no matter where it's hiding. I want all inside doors wide open, all windows and outside doors locked, and all curtains closed."

A feeling of intense cold suddenly swept over me, and I glanced uneasily at the others. Mum shivered involuntarily. "I'll go and do it," she said, hurrying upstairs. I swear an unholy chuckle rang faintly down the passage. I peered into the thickening shadows. Nothing stirred.

The vicar looked at Dad. "There's something here alright. Something that doesn't belong. I'll start as soon as your wife's back. We must get it out of the house at once."

"No!" The word was conjured from empty air, strong and throaty. As the dreadful sound died away, the lounge door slammed shut and the hall curtains suddenly billowed outwards like great balloons.

The Reverend McBeil's eyes widened and he swallowed fiercely, looking as if he were trying to control an outburst of emotion.

"Hurry, Mrs. Reynolds," he shouted up the stairs. "I must start. Hurry, please. We'll be a stronger force when we're all together." I started to move towards the lounge door, but he caught my arm. "No. Leave it closed. It doesn't matter now we've cornered it."

"Cornered me!" The contemptuous roar echoed from every vestige of the hall. "You can't stop me taking what's rightfully mine."

"But what is rightfully yours?" I cried desperately. "What do you want?"

I saw the vicar's mouth open and caught the warning look on his face, but his words were lost, carried away on a sudden, gusting wind. A wind in our house—with the doors and windows closed. It didn't make sense, but it was happening nonetheless.

The curtains lashed into a violent frenzy, tugging at the rings securing them to the rail, eager to be free. The leaves of the plant on the telephone table danced wildly under the unrelenting touch of the wind whistling and howling around us. Suddenly the potted plant was lifted by the gale's invisible hand and sent crashing to the floor.

Then the mirror on the wall raised off its hook and hurtled through the air towards the vicar. He, like the rest of us, was rooted to the spot, unable to move as the heavy gilt-edged mirror flew for his head, homing in fast on its target with unnerving accuracy. He let out a yell at the last second and flung himself sideways. The mirror shot past within an inch of his head and crashed sickeningly into the stairs, casting hundreds of shards of glass in all directions.

The girls' long hair streamed out; Sarah's behind her as she faced the wind, Helen's in front as she stood with her back to it. Sarah battled to reach Helen, finally clamping her arm round her sister's neck and burying her head deep in Helen's shoulder.

Their tears were dried by the wind's incredible power almost before they left their eyes. It was like a hurricane, making it nigh on impossible for us to stand.

The whistling and howling grew with each passing second, as did the feeling of intense unease and horror. It was the same feeling our visitor had brought with it on its nightly dashes past the window, which seemed so tame compared to what was happening now.

Relentlessly the unearthly wind battered us, freezing me to the very marrow. I knew we couldn't face it for long. The vicar's voice was harsh and husky as he fought to be heard over the noise. "We need to start," he yelled. "It's getting more powerful all the time. Into the lounge, quickly."

But that was easier said than done. In a flash the wind changed direction. Its source now appeared to be the lounge door. One second the hall curtains were billowing out, the next they were pressed flat like a skin over the window panes.

I threw my arms around the girls and the three of us, bent double to cut the fierce resistance, thrust out towards the door as the wind howled deafeningly in my ears. Dad staggered towards the vicar at the bottom of the stairs and the two of them huddled together amidst the shattered remnants of the mirror

"Jean," Dad shouted up the stairs. "Where are you?"

Looking up, I saw Mum appear on the landing. "Whatever's happening down there?"

"Be careful. It's. . . " The rest of Dad's words were drowned to a whisper as the wind whistled about us and finally whisked Dad and the Reverend McBeil off their feet. They thudded down onto the stairs, their hands and faces crashing into the jagged pieces of glass. Then it bowled up the stairs, flattening Mum into the far wall.

Now free of the gale, I sprang into action, hauling the lounge door open and thrusting the girls inside.

I realised too late that the lounge was an inferno. I couldn't believe my eyes: the girls tumbled into the room as flames and thick acrid smoke snaked out like grasping tentacles to snatch them into its very heart. In a desperate effort to reach the girls, I plunged headlong through the blazing doorway. Something caught my foot and I toppled and sprawled to the floor. The girls screamed hysterically, and as I pulled my face from the carpet wondering what horrors would meet my sight next, a pair of arms materialised through the flames and plucked Helen away, back through the door.

And there was the voice again. "Come back to me," it cried as Helen shot from view, obliterated by the choking smoke. Sarah clasped her hands around her ears, shaking her head frantically from side to side as the fire twisted and turned its way over her clothes.

As the initial shock dissipated and I hauled myself up onto my elbows, my eyes widened with a peculiar realisation: although the flames had touched all three of us we were not burned; the flames were without heat. Our clothes, our bodies, were unmarked. So was the furniture, which, had this been an ordinary fire, would have long since burned. I remembered that night in Mark's bedroom. "This isn't real," I screamed at the top of my voice. "The flames aren't burning anything."

Suddenly the flames were no longer there. They retracted into the floor and walls, taking the wind with them; everything was quiet and tranquil in an instant.

Helen lay a metre from the door. Who had snatched her from those harmless flames? It couldn't have been Dad or the vicar, who were dizzily picking themselves up off the glass-strewn floor with blood trickling from their cheeks and the palms of their hands. While I stood watching from the doorway, they staggered towards Helen. I set off as well, and we reached her at the same time. Mum ran downstairs, sobbing, and we huddled together in a small, frightened group. We looked round at the shattered hall that had suddenly become still, the calm only broken by rhythmical sobs from Mum and Helen, and Sarah, who was still in the lounge.

The vicar looked around feverishly for his candle and Bible, which he'd dropped as he struggled to keep upright in the first onslaught of that unnatural wind.

"We must exorcise this evil now." His voice held a strange timbre, and he looked drawn and haggard. Even though he was visibly shaking as well, an imposing quality still managed to radiate from him. I felt great faith in the elderly man. If anyone could free us from this terrible curse, he could.

He retrieved his candle and Bible with a trembling hand. "Quickly. Matches. We must begin straight away. I need matches to light the candle." As Dad reached into his pocket to pull out the box he used for lighting his pipe, I noticed his hand was streaked with blood from a myriad of tiny cuts. The vicar seemed to almost snatch the matches from his grasp and clumsily open the box.

"We must be quick," he muttered as he took one out and struck it firmly against the rough edge. It crackled but failed to ignite. He rubbed again. This time the pink head of the match dissolved in a tiny explosion of flame. After transferring its light- and heat-giving tip to the wick, he watched with evident satisfaction as the candle came alive in a strong, perfect nozzle of fire.

I hurried into the lounge and returned with my arms cradled comfortingly around Sarah's shoulders. "Come on," I whispered soothingly into her long blonde hair. "It'll soon be over. The vicar's going to get rid of it." Deep in my heart I prayed that those words that sprang so easily to my lips wouldn't prove to be a lie. The night was proving to be more than anyone could stand. This had to be the end. It just had to be.

The vicar's crisp, confident tones snapped me to attention. "Mr. Reynolds, Simon, come stand next to me, please. Everyone else, behind me." I swiftly flanked his left arm and Dad his right, while Mum and the girls cowered behind us. We turned in a solid group to face the stairs.

"Quickly," said the vicar. "Make the sign of the cross with your two forefingers." We did as he ordered and I noticed that the crucifix resting on his chest, hanging from a silver chain, appeared to reflect the light in a most peculiar fashion. The whole of the cross was pulsating with a miscellany of vivid colour. One moment it was blue, the next red, then green. His right arm shot out towards the stairs, the Bible firmly grasped in his sweating fingers.

He thrust out his left hand, too. The candle flame bent back towards him for a second or two.

His words crashed through the air like a thunderbolt. "I call on the love of Jesus Christ to banish you from this house. And I call upon him to protect us this night from your power. Begone, back to the realms of darkness from where you came."

He was interrupted by a fierce grunt that seemed to emanate from thin air halfway up the stairs—or was it halfway down? Was it getting closer? Stronger?

A half-strangled, almost pathetic cry rent the air. "Everything is here. Don't stop me now," it said.

"Away with you, spawn of Satan. You come from the devil's own abode. Go back now, before I call on the power and love of Jesus Christ to shatter your very being, your very spirit, into the oblivion of a thousand pieces."

I felt confident that the Reverend McBeil had taken command. Our deadly foe was on the run, on the defensive. Surely now it would only be a matter of time.

A fierce pounding began on the stairs, as if a giant hammer were being thrust up and down on the carpet. Its echo rang madly throughout the hall, vibrant and powerful, and a cloud of smoke somewhat reminiscent of the dying embers of a bonfire sprang up to mask the step beyond. The smoke was white and appeared to be taking on a definite shape. It was as if each shred of smoke knew its place and was becoming interwoven with its neighbour to take on a solid form.

As we looked on in absolute terror, the white billowing mass drifted up the stairs to the landing where it stopped dead. At first it simply stood there, as if it were looking down on us, mocking, knowing its strength. More smoke seemed to grow from its very bowels, and before long a six-foot human form towered there. It was indistinct, without features, but where the eyes should be were two burning red holes, as if we were looking into hell itself. Those eyes mirrored all the wickedness and evil ever born on this earth—and yet, at the same time, I sensed a deep and bitter sadness that lay beyond. The smoke moved subtly, but without any real change. The sadness seemed to take over. The evil was replaced by a haunted, longing look from within those burning holes.

"You can't fool us." The Reverend McBeil's words were strong and majestic. Still the fierce pounding hammered into my ears, this time from the top of the stairs where the entity stood. There was no movement, yet the noise grew in strength, pounding ever deeper into my head. I screwed my face up, trying to be rid of the hurtful, hateful sound, but still it persisted, driving onwards, deep and penetrating.

Behind me Sarah screamed and I sensed, rather than saw, her withdraw her handmade cross to cover her ears.

"No," yelled the vicar. "Keep the sign of the cross. Don't weaken our power." But it was too late. The second Sarah dropped her hands from the position of the cross the white misty figure at the top of the stairs took the next step toward becoming solid. The bedroom door behind it became dimmer as the smoke thickened. The intolerable noise—the thumping, the banging, the hammering, the unholy sound of hell itself—drove on ever louder. My head pounded, pushing me to copy Sarah, to cover my ears in a feeble effort to drown the evil sound, but I knew I must resist.

Still the creature stood there, mocking, as if daring us to let it live.

The inner voice, given life by our foe on the stairs, spoke to me again, doing its best to fight my efforts to resist it. *Let me come*, it cried. *Don't oppose me. Give me what's mine. Sleep. Sleep. Sleep. Let go your cross.*

It was almost as if I could sense the creature's inner turmoil and its frantic attempts to defeat us. Its cry became a roar, battering the inside of my head as I held out against its power, and I sent back a defiant message of my own. "You're not going to win. Leave us alone!"

I don't know how long we persevered against it, but Mum was next to weaken. "I can't stand it anymore," she sobbed. "Please stop. Please, please, please." Her voice, shrill and loud, cut through the thunderous roar, and as I glanced round I saw her break the sign of the cross and clasp her ears.

"No" I cried. "Don't give in to it."

"Keep the sign of the cross." The Reverend McBeil's voice was harsh and insistent. "It's the only defence we have at the moment."

The creature's triumphant laugh was something that will be with me to my dying day, and something I never wanted to hear again.

The power of the smoky, white figure grew with the loss of another of our defences. A further bitter, twisted laugh escaped from where its lips should have been. And then slowly a mouth began to grow in its face. Features began to form, vaguely, but they were definitely moulding.

White, wispy arms raised themselves in an all-embracing gesture. The noise became even more deafening and the lights flickered. Then, above the din, I heard the whistling of the wind in the distance. It was coming again. Slowly, like a breeze tickling the leaves on a summer's day, it wafted around my face before it was suddenly back, as strong and powerful as it had been moments earlier.

The candle flame blew and twisted, bending low under the force of the wind. Suddenly it shot up, mighty and high, fierce and bright, rocketing a good two metres into the air. That small and meagre half-inch wick burst into a wondrous flame, dancing madly between us and the source of its newfound power on the stairs, just for a second. Then the flame thinned to the thickness of a piece of string, hurtled itself from the wick up the stairs, dividing itself into two as it went. Each strand of fire reached the outstretched hands of the monstrous being and plunged deep within them. As they did so, the creature grew in stature, strength, and power. The lights flickered again, then dimmed. Soon they'd be gone altogether and we'd be in darkness, just us and this monster from the pit. It would be in its element.

Each time the lights faltered the white smoke grew thicker and the wind became stronger. As before, we had to bend into it or be knocked backwards. In order to keep my sign of the cross I dropped to my knees and tucked my head onto my shoulder, but still the wind tore round me and still the hammering persisted, thumping ceaselessly and relentlessly.

The lights gave up without warning as the power that was draining them finally won. Pure energy shot from the bulbs across the hall and up the stairs, finding their target in the outstretched arms. Sudden, intense darkness surrounded us; the only light came from the figure at the top of the stairs, which now radiated and glowed with the energy stolen from us.

The creature's lips split into a hollow grin as it finally started down the stairs towards us, its face becoming more distinct with every step.

"I command you. . ." The Reverend McBeil's voice strained above the wind that kept us bowed down. "Go back from whence you came, you creature of darkness. In the name of our Lord Jesus Christ, begone!"

Somewhere beyond the dreadful roar of the gale and constant hammering, I heard the crashing of our hall furniture as the wind picked it up like matchwood and smashed it against the walls. Yet still the vicar's words cut through.

The light shining from the creature grew brighter as it came closer, casting an eerie, almost moonlight-like glow across the hall. The vicar stood upright, his hair skinned back from his head in the blast of the hurricane. The creature took another step. Slowly the white smoke solidified. And there on the stairs stood a human man, as firm and real as any I have ever seen. Tall, thin, brown-eyed, with black hair cut short and swept back off the forehead. Behind me, Helen screamed. As I turned she, too, dropped her crossed fingers. Her eyes were wide and staring as she gazed upon the spirit's face. "You!" The single word tore from Helen's lips in a terrified shriek.

Something drew my eyes to the vicar's face that was contorting beyond belief as he shook his head, trying to pretend it wasn't happening. The next second the contortions disappeared and a determined look engulfed him. "Die, you monstrous thing. Die." The lifeless candle dropped from his grasp and he tore the crucifix from around his neck. With one movement, he hurled the Bible from his right hand and the cross from his left, straight into the advancing form. In an instant, the malicious smirk disappeared from the creature's face as, with an agonised cry, it thrust up its hands to where the makeshift missiles had passed through. The movement was accompanied by a blinding flash and deafening roar, and I was buffeted by this new power surge. Sprawling backwards into Mum and the girls, my last conscious memory was of the most dreadful scream coming from the thing on the stairs. I tried to look up to see what the creature was doing, but dropped suddenly into peaceful oblivion.

It must have been only a second or two at most before I awoke. Pitch-blackness surrounded me before the discarded candle burst into life, its flame rekindled. But the only thing going through my mind was that inhuman cry of pain and despair I heard before I passed out.

I struggled into a slumped position and looked around. The power of the candle's flame was now immense as it shone far and wide, illuminating the entire hall. I shook my head vigorously to clear it and found I could still hear the lingering throbs of that terrible cry. As the echoes died away, so did the flickering flame until it was nothing more than an ordinary candle again. The electric light found a new lease on life in that same moment, coming back and flooding the scene with brightness.

The creature was gone.

A series of harsh coughs escaped Dad's lips, sounding as if their birth had been deep in the pit of his stomach. I looked across to him on the other side of the vicar and saw that between coughs he was breathing heavily, his head thrown back as he gasped to take in air, and his eyes stared upwards. He slowly brought his outstretched arms down, fingers still in the sign of the cross. Sarah and Mum lay in separate heaps on the floor, light sobs slipping from their throats. Helen stood as she had before that cry had been wrenched from her mouth. Her eyes were glazed, staring, yet unseeing. The next moment her legs crumpled as she toppled to the floor in a faint.

The vicar seemed immobile, but only for a fraction of a second. Then he leaped forward in great bounds up the stairs to gather his Bible and crucifix. "Look at this," he cried triumphantly, holding them aloft. "We've done it. The spirit has gone. The cross and Bible have banished it."

I drank in his words eagerly, their power swimming dizzily through my mind. Was it true? Could we possibly have destroyed this thing from hell that plagued us?

Dad turned to where Helen lay on the floor and whisked her up into his arms. Mum and Sarah comforted each other, sitting with their backs pressed against the wall and gripping each other's hands. The vicar waited until Dad had carried Helen upstairs and along the corridor

towards her room before starting down slowly. When he got to the
bottom, he silently held out the Bible, crucifix, and chain for me to
examine. Scorch marks scarred the cover of the holy book and the once-
shining crucifix was dull and tarnished as if both had been passed
through fire.

"Is it really over. . .truly?" sobbed Mum, the fingers of her free
hand kneading Sarah's shoulder in the same way people played with
worry beads.

The Reverend McBeil nodded as a couple drops of sweat trickled
between his eyebrows and down his nose. "Don't you feel it?" he asked
quietly. "The sense of peace and tranquillity?" He looked across at me
and I handed him his Bible and crucifix. "It's that feeling of emptiness I
spoke about the other day. Whatever it was, whatever it wanted, it's
gone now."

"It was a man," whispered Sarah.

"And we'll never know what it wanted." I returned the vicar's
gaze. "I would have liked to know, after all we've been through."

"Just be thankful it's gone," said Mum as she climbed to her feet,
pulling Sarah up. "I'd better go and help your Dad with Helen."

"It's okay," came Dad's voice from the top of the stairs. "She's
sleeping like a log."

"Do you think we should call a doctor?"

The vicar shook his head and smoothed down his disarrayed
hair. "No. Let her sleep until morning. She'll be fine."

"Is it safe for us to stay the night now?" asked Dad as he came
downstairs.

"Yes, the spirit's gone. There's nothing more to worry about." The
vicar sighed wearily. "I'm tired. I'd better be getting back home."

"Do stay and have a drink with us," Mum insisted, but the vicar
shook his head.

"At least a coffee?"

"Thank you, Mrs. Reynolds, but no. You'll want to be alone tonight."

Dad laughed. "That's the last thing we want at the moment."

"No, no. Once you've got your breath back and sit down to
examine what's happened you'll be glad I left." He gripped my arm,
leading me aside. "Do come and see me tomorrow, Simon. You may
need my guidance."

"Guidance?" I queried.

"You may want to talk over what's happened, and perhaps more importantly, why it's happened. I want to explain how the power and love of Jesus Christ was able to overcome adversaries like this. Please call on me tomorrow."

Dad dropped the vicar off at the vicarage, and Helen was still sleeping soundly when we all turned in a couple of hours later. It was true what the Reverend McBeil had said; the house did seem less claustrophobic, somehow cleaner, brighter, purer. But I could not rid myself of the dreadful scenes we had witnessed. And try as I might, I could not completely believe it was finally over.

CHAPTER 16: THE RETURN

I LAY AWAKE tossing and turning as the final moments of Sunday night merged with those of Monday morning. I kept seeing that face with its foreboding eyes and swept-back hair. The more I thought about it the stronger its presence came back to me, as if it were still hiding darkly and deeply in every corner and recess the house provided, lurking, waiting, watching, snuggling in the warmth. In shadows waiting.

Eventually sleep washed over me, but instead of bringing relief from my waking thoughts it only served to accentuate them, turning them into nightmarish monsters. I felt small and vulnerable, expecting to feel it pressing against me at any moment, trying to get under the duvet to engulf me in its cloying grip. Titus, who'd sprouted wings of flaming orange and a tail that ended in a wickedly sharp barb like a scorpion's stinger, chased a giant green-winged cat across my dreamscape.

Helen's smiling face drifted into view, but before I could smile back it dissolved into a snarling, spitting tiger, which, in turn, became Mark Brody. And Mark was humming softly to himself. A soothing melodious tune. The sound was heavenly, totally out of this world and I listened entranced. It was the music of angels.

The humming grew in pitch and intensity, and as I lay spellbound Mark's face transformed into a clock, its hands showing quarter past four. Suddenly I was looking at my bedside clock radio, which showed the same time. The humming was getting louder all the time, developing steadily into a terrifying siren. I wanted the noise to stop.

Across my bedroom I could see another bed that wasn't quite solid but instead was wispy and transparent. Two people, who also weren't quite solid, were sleeping in it. I looked around feverishly. This wasn't my bedroom. The curtains that were drawn tightly across to prevent even the slightest shaft of light from lancing out into the darkness weren't my curtains. The carpet on the floor wasn't my carpet. The wardrobes weren't my wardrobes. None of it seemed quite real or solid. There was something ethereal about it, and I could see the wallpaper through everything quite clearly. But it wasn't my wallpaper.

Apart from all that, it *was* my bedroom.

How it could be.

How it might have been once.

How it *was* once.

The siren droned on outside but not loud enough to drown the sound of aeroplanes high above. Suddenly the girl in the bed opposite sat bolt upright, her back to me as she shook the man's shoulders violently. I watched with incredulity as he too sat up, his face obscured by the girl. She put her hands to her ears, clasping them tightly to kill the interminable row of the siren. She shook her head from side to side, hands still at her ears, her long blond hair tumbling in uncontrollable cascades around her shoulders.

When I tried to leap out of bed to comfort her I realised I couldn't move. I was sitting up in bed in my room—*no. Not my room*—and I couldn't move a muscle. All I could do was watch helplessly as the scene played out around me—and it was real. This was no stage-bound drama and I the audience. It was happening before my very eyes. I saw the girl jump out of bed and run in her nightdress to the door. By the time I looked from her to the man, I could only see his back as he fled after her into the corridor.

The instant the door swung shut behind them I was free of whatever unseen chains held me immobile against the bed. With one spring I was across to the door, my hands gripped the handle, twisting, pulling, pushing, turning—but I couldn't get the door to yield. It was shut firmly and stayed shut as if locked. I tugged for several seconds but the door wouldn't budge. I was trapped in my bedroom. *No. Not my room.*

And the noise. The intolerable noise. The humming had become a high-pitched whistling. I ran to the window and pulled back the curtains. Flames streamed before my eyes. The whole sky seemed on fire, one huge mass of orange and smoke. The village itself appeared to be ablaze, and over the treetops I could see the flames as they leaped into the night sky, casting an eerie glow on everything around them the night the bomb fell on White Pastures in the final days of the war.

The whistling became more intense, nearer, louder as the bomb fell lower and lower. I hammered on the window, desperately trying to shout a warning to the girl who by now was running across the lawn. But she gave no indication of hearing me. I tried to open the window, but it refused to move. It was shut firmly and wouldn't give an inch. I looked up and fancied I caught a glimpse of the falling shell glinting against the moon. There, below, the girl in her nightdress ran barefoot to her doom. And I was helpless in my bedroom—*no. In her bedroom*—unable to stop her.

By now her husband was on the edge of the lawn, his head raised heavenward as he too saw the falling bomb, which was only a few dozen metres above the trees at the bottom of the garden. His garden. My garden.

Then the bomb was down and everything else was up. High up in the air. Trees, or rather torn shattered fragments of trees, were up in the air, grass and earth were up in the air. And the shrill, penetrating whistle was replaced by the roar of a deafening, ear-splitting explosion.

Somehow that terrible scene of long ago was being replayed in front of me. The drama had almost reached its conclusion. The young girl, Jim Roberts's bride, was about to meet her death on the grounds of White Pastures. The whole house shook around me as I watched Jim Roberts throw himself to the ground, his hands protectively around his head.

And the last thing I saw before the glass shattered in front of my eyes was the girl being flung in the air like a rag doll. In mid-flight, the force of the impact whipped her round, and her horrified face turned agonisingly towards me in the last split second of her life. And I saw her features for the first time.

Her face, her broken, smashed, and bloody body, spanned the years as she tumbled and twisted. The explosion rang in my ears and as I threw my hands up to protect my eyes from the thousands of shards of flying glass, I was knocked backwards by the force of the blast.

But that fraction of a second when I saw her face was enough. There was no doubt I had been looking straight into the terrified face of my own sister, Helen.

The sound died away. The silence, the overwhelming quietness, echoed unnaturally in my soul. I lay there for a few seconds on the floor where I'd been blown by the force of the explosion before I heard the door open and a scream stung my ears.

Sarah stood framed in the doorway, the very doorway that only moments earlier had refused to yield to me. She must have touched the switch, because light instantly flooded the room. I looked around tentatively. The curtains were drawn back, waving erratically, and the window lay in shattered glass fragments on the floor. The curtains' dancing movements stilled. Nothing stirred. Sarah didn't move. Her hands covered her nose and mouth. Eyes wide open. She was rooted to the spot.

Then I realised that hers hadn't been the only scream. Before she'd torn down the passage to my bedroom I'd been aware of a more agonised scream from elsewhere in the house.

I hadn't been able to hear the girl outside when she screamed, although I'll never forget the sight of that silent cry working its way up to her lips when she felt the deadly breath of the explosion. But it was Helen's voice that had screamed the horrible, unnatural death knell as I was blown backwards onto the floor. And the scream came from the depths of White Pastures. From Helen's bedroom.

Mum suddenly appeared in the doorway beside Sarah. She was hysterical, her hands too were up to her face and she was stamping each foot in turn in a sort of peculiar little dance. When she saw me there, amidst the splinters of my window, her hands slid slowly down her cheeks and over her chin, and her legs buckled beneath her before she dropped onto the landing carpet.

I hardly had time to get up and pick carefully through the glass before Dad appeared.

"What the devil's going on?" he yelled, seeing the devastation in my bedroom.

"Helen. See to Helen. See that she's alright," I shouted as I made my way through the maze of glass splinters that threatened my bare feet if I misplaced a step.

Dad didn't come back. I was still comforting Sarah and Mum when he called my name. Until that moment only Sarah's sobs broke the stillness, and I realised that the house had been insanely quiet. One second I was at the window looking out on a scene of long ago, then that scene had been obliterated, overtaken by events in the here and now.

"Simon! For God's sake! Simon!" The agony in Dad's voice was unmistakable as it rang out from Helen's bedroom.

Leaving Sarah to look after Mum, I ran down the passage to find Dad kneeling on the floor beside Helen's bed, his hand gripped tightly around hers, pressing it to his lips, his head bowed. He turned towards me, his whole body trembling. I looked down at the form lying motionless beneath the rumpled bedclothes.

Tears rolled down Dad's cheeks. I had to listen carefully to make any sense of the listless, whispered words that were coming between his wrenching sobs.

"My God, Simon. . . my God. She's dead."

CHAPTER 17: REVELATION

THE DOCTOR CAME OUT of Mum's room and pulled the door shut behind him. "She's resting now. She'll be fine physically in a couple of days." He looked at me strangely. "It's a form of shock brought on by Helen's death." Then he paused, as if expecting me to say something. When I remained silent he had no option but to continue. "She kept saying she heard a peculiar noise, like an old wartime air raid siren, then a whistling and an explosion of some sort."

I felt myself sweating, hoping he wouldn't see the beads of moisture trickling down my brow. The bomb hadn't been a dream. At least not *just* a dream.

Shaking my head slowly, I held his quizzical gaze. "She's just confused, isn't she? With the shock of seeing Helen like that?"

It was a moment or so before he spoke. "And what about Helen? That look on her face? It was as if she died of fright."

"But I thought you said it was a heart attack?"

"I'm sure that's what the post mortem will show. But the heart attack was caused by something."

What the doctor said was true. But how could we tell him Helen had died from events at the end of World War II that had somehow been reenacted down the corridors of time?

The look of sheer terror on Helen's face was something I never wanted to see again, but which I knew my mind's eye would see every moment for the rest of my life. Her twisted features were just pale flesh pulled grotesquely around a bony framework.

"Doctor, I'm sure you'll excuse us now." Dad's tone was firm; he needn't say more.

Later, as the sun rose heralding the dawn of a day Helen would never see, I began to turn over in my mind what the doctor said after examining Mum. It seemed she'd heard the bomb too. It must have truly happened exactly as I saw it. Time had come round again across the years.

*   *   *

A few hours later I was back at the vicarage. The Reverend McBeil was stunned to learn what had happened after he left. He put his head in his hands, and didn't look up for a full five minutes. He appeared lost in some deep private grief; the news seemed to destroy him.

I felt I had to let him make the first move, and my heart felt heavier than ever as I sat there in his study. This was the first time I'd witnessed any human death, let alone that of a close family member, and it seemed that the hollow, empty feeling in the pit of my stomach would never go away. My limbs and mind felt totally numb.

When he eventually raised his head, his eyes were moist behind the dark-rimmed glasses and tears slowly rolled down each cheek.

"I'm so sorry, Simon. So very, very sorry."

I nodded dumbly. What could I say to him? "Yes, well, it's. . ."

"I could've prevented it, you know. I could have warned you."

"Don't blame yourself, Vicar. We all thought the spirit had gone."

"I don't mean that. It's something else entirely. A long—"

"You said we might need your help and guidance," I continued, only half-hearing his words and not completely aware that I had interrupted him. "I've never felt that the church could help me before. But now I—"

"Please, Simon, I must explain to you." He lowered his head again. "If only I'd realised—fully realised—I could've stopped all this and Helen would still be alive."

"But Vicar, you can't blame yourself."

"Oh, can't I? There's more to this than you know or understand, my boy, and what happened last night only goes to confirm my own foolishness. Whether it was a dream or reenactment of that terrible night when young Heidi was killed, it could've been stopped. *I could have stopped it.*"

My thoughts were on a track of their own, overriding what he was saying.

"Do you really think that somehow I was able to see back in time?" I asked. "That I was actually watching it happen?" A sudden notion struck me. "Vicar, did you live here then, when Meriton was bombed?"

"I did. I've lived in the village all my life. Heidi's death, coming just after her wedding, robbed me of all the fire I'd had in my belly to get out into the world and do God's work. I figured that if God could allow something like that to happen, my work would best be carried out here." His sobs came in bursts. "And now I've let it happen again."

I was only half-hearing what he was saying and my level of understanding was even less. My train of thought was focused on something else entirely. "You don't by any chance remember the time of the bombing, do you?"

"As clearly as if it were yesterday. It's etched on my mind forever. Quarter past four. I can still see that clock when the air raid siren woke me and I was ushered out with everyone else in the family to the Anderson shelter. It was. . ."

I was no longer hearing him at all. My mind was back to the dream when the clock sprang from Mark's face, back to my bedside clock radio, back to the numerous occasions I'd found myself awake recently at that precise moment.

Silently he pulled the bottom drawer of his desk open and brought out a frayed newspaper cutting. I took the proffered cutting, which was yellowing with age. The photograph and words on it were plainly visible.

My heart leaped. It was a wedding report cut from the local newspaper, and the two happy, smiling faces staring up at me from across the years were those of my sister Helen and the apparition I'd seen at the top of the stairs. There was no mistaking the man. The short haircut swept neatly away from the high forehead, the deep brown eyes. Every feature was the same.

"James Roberts and Heidi Ryknield," said the vicar. "They were the first couple I ever married. It was just about the first church work I did here. Then she died a few days after that picture was taken and her husband disappeared."

My eyes were glued to the girl's face in the ageing photo, unsuccessfully searching for something that would tell me it wasn't Helen.

"What did happen to him?" I asked, trying not to let a tremor creep into my voice.

"After Heidi's funeral he set off to walk home and wouldn't let anyone go with him. As you know, it's only a couple of miles from the church to White Pastures, but somewhere along that route Jim Roberts disappeared from the face of the earth and was never seen again. It was widely thought he killed himself, but his body was never found."

Oh, he has been seen again, I thought. *Back at his house—our house—or at least what's left of him. His soul, his spirit, has been back to reclaim his bride.*

"You'll probably think me a silly old man for telling you this," said the Reverend McBeil, "But I had a dream a few nights after Heidi's funeral, such a vivid dream that I've never forgotten it. I'd just gone to bed and must have been exhausted because it all seemed to happen as soon as I'd put the light out. I must have gone to sleep immediately. In my dream I was sitting up in bed when a dark shadow appeared in the corner of the room. It grew from a shapeless mass to a vaguely human form. It became more distinct every second and I could soon see its face quite clearly. As I stared at it, it spoke to me. There was no mistaking either the face or the voice. It was Jim Roberts. At first I thought I must be awake and he'd clambered up the vines outside my bedroom window. But as he spoke, the shadow dimmed and faded away before my eyes. I remember trying to snap myself awake, and the next moment I was sitting up in bed shivering with a definite chill in the air that hadn't been there before."

"You said Jim Roberts spoke to you that night?"

He nodded silently, almost as if he couldn't bring himself to tell me any more. I was forced to ask what the apparition had said.

I could tell by the look on the Reverend McBeil's face that he was thinking back in time. "I can remember his exact words." He paused again, looking me straight in the eyes, causing a shiver to emerge in the small of my back.

"He said to me, 'Reverend McBeil, you have married us in the house of the Lord. In the eyes of God, Heidi and I are one, bound to each other with a ring of gold. Nothing shall put us asunder. One day I will return for my bride.'"

"But if. . .?" Thoughts whirled irrationally through my muddled mind. "I don't understand. If James Roberts did kill himself wouldn't he have been with Heidi again?"

The vicar shrugged. "I can't offer any explanation, Simon. I'm merely telling you what I know. One thing I might say, though, is that suicide is regarded as a major sin against God. If, in fact, he did kill himself, maybe his spirit has been condemned to wander in limbo all these years. Who knows?"

"But why take my sister? Unless. . .?" My eyes dropped to the photograph. "Do you believe in reincarnation?"

This time he smiled. "As a believer in the Christian faith, I must say no, I don't. I believe in the final resurrection of man, and until the final day of judgement is upon us the spirit dwells elsewhere, not in another body."

Clearly, though, his voice lacked sincerity, and his eyes clouded as if he knew the spark of truth had gone.

I had just reached the door when he called me back. "There is perhaps one more thing you should know, Simon," he said. "Heidi Roberts died the night after her twentieth birthday."

CHAPTER 18: ASCENSION

AND SO the dark cloud ascended from us. We were free of it at last. But what a price we paid.

The spirit only wanted its own true love back, and in its sad and misguided way it had seen in my dear sister the happiness it lost all those years ago.

I don't suppose we shall ever know whether Helen really was the reincarnation of poor Heidi, or if she was just an innocent victim caught in a dreadful spiritual mix-up.

But quite often in my dreams and in my mind's eye I see them: Jim and Heidi hand in hand, wandering wherever it is contented souls go.

Happy and peaceful.

Reunited.

Across the years.

THE END

ABOUT THE AUTHOR

Stewart Bint is a magazine columnist and PR writer. He lives with his wife, Sue, in Leicestershire in the UK and has two children, Christopher and Charlotte.

As a member of a local barefoot hiking group, when not writing he can often be found hiking barefoot on woodland trails.

CONNECT WITH STEWART BINT ONLINE:

Website:

stewartbintauthor.weebly.com

Blog:

stewartbintauthor.weebly.com/stewart-bints-blog

Twitter:

twitter.com/@AuthorSJB

Facebook:

en-gb.facebook.com/people/Stewart-Bint

MORE GREAT READS FROM BOOKTROPE

Blood & Spirits by **Dennis Sharpe** (Paranormal) Small-town life can be hard for a dead girl. A raucous ride through the dangerous lives of the lecherous undead.

Inhuman Interest by **Eric Turowski** (Paranormal Thriller) Tess Cooper's world turns upside down after the mysterious Davin Egypt reveals a world of occult forces beyond human comprehension.

Fall of Knight by **Steven Cross** (Paranormal) Social abuse, bullying and mental illness are just some of the problems Dean Knight deals with on an everyday basis. And then there's the monster.

No Shelter from Darkness by **Mark D. Evans** (Paranormal) In the post-Blitz East End of London, orphaned teenager Beth Wade is bullied for looking different. But it goes far deeper than looks. With a growing thirst for blood and the arrival of a man who could kill her just as easily as help her, Beth must fight for control of her life . . . and of herself.

Touched by **A.J. Aalto** (Paranormal) The media has a nickname for Marnie Baranuik, though she'd rather they didn't; they call her the Great White Shark. A forensic psychic twice-touched by the Blue Sense, which gives her the ability to feel the emotions of others and read impressions left behind on objects, Marnie is too mean to die young, backed up by friends in cold places, and has a mouth as demure as a cannon's blast.

Netherworld by **K.N. Lee** (Paranormal Fantasy) The Netherworld Division are an organization of angels and humans who are there to keep the escaped creatures from The Netherworld in check.

Organ Reapers by **Shay West** (Paranormal Fiction) A series of gruesome and mysterious killings with no viable evidence or eyewitnesses force detectives Robinson and Aguilar to search outside their realm of experience...and into another dimension.

The Soul Thief by **Majanka Verstraete** (Paranormal Fiction) 16-year-old Riley must come to terms with being a Halfling Angel of Death while battling an evil force that has murdered several girls her age, knowing she'll be next...

Discover more books and learn about our
new approach to publishing at **booktrope.com**.

Lightning Source UK Ltd.
Milton Keynes UK
UKOW04f2213301115

263811UK00002B/103/P

9 781620 158340